Lucy Pauline Hobart

The Changed Cross

And other Religious Poems

Lucy Pauline Hobart

The Changed Cross
And other Religious Poems

ISBN/EAN: 9783744771177

Printed in Europe, USA, Canada, Australia, Japan

Cover: Foto ©Andreas Hilbeck / pixelio.de

More available books at **www.hansebooks.com**

THE

CHANGED CROSS,

AND

OTHER RELIGIOUS POEMS.

New Edition.

LONDON:

SAMPSON LOW, MARSTON, SEARLE, & RIVINGTON,
LIMITED,
St. Dunstan's House,
FETTER LANE, FLEET STREET, E.C.
GLASGOW: J. N. MACKINLAY.
1888.

Ballantyne Press
BALLANTYNE, HANSON AND CO.
EDINBURGH AND LONDON

THIS little collection of sacred poetry has originated in a desire to give permanent form to a few waifs and strays of great merit, appearing in newspapers and magazines. As a collection, the publication first appeared in New York, where it obtained much favour; subsequently, in an enlarged edition, it has attracted the regard of many English admirers, for whom it is now reprinted. In a few instances the names or initials of the writers have become known by their subsequent reputation as poets; but to preserve the original idea and connecting link of the collection, it has been deemed better to reprint the book as it appeared in 1865.

October 1870.

———

OWING to the many mistakes which have arisen with reference to the authorship of the poem which gives the title to this little volume, it is necessary to state that it was written some years ago by the Honourable Mrs. Charles Hobart (*née* L. P. W.). and is published by her sanction.

May 1873.

THE CHANGED CROSS,

AND

OTHER RELIGIOUS POEMS.

—◦—

IT was a time of sadness, and my heart,
    Although it knew and loved the better part,
Felt wearied with the conflict and the strife,
And all the needful discipline of life.

And while I thought on these, as given to me—
My trial tests of faith and love to be—
It seemed as if I never could be sure
That faithful to the end I should endure.

And thus, no longer trusting to His might
Who says, "We walk by faith, and not by
    sight,"
Doubting, and almost yielding to despair,
The thought arose—My cross I cannot bear:

Far heavier its weight must surely be
Than those of others which I daily see.
Oh! if I might another burden choose,
Methinks I should not fear my crown to lose.

A solemn silence reigned on all around—
E'en Nature's voices uttered not a sound;
The evening shadows seemed of peace to tell,
And sleep upon my weary spirit fell.

A moment's pause—and then a heavenly light
Beamed full upon my wondering, raptured
    sight;
Angels on silvery wings seemed everywhere,
And angels' music thrilled the balmy air.

Then One, more fair than all the rest to see—
One to whom all the others bowed the knee—
Came gently to me as I trembling lay,
And, "Follow me!" He said; "I am the
    Way."

Then, speaking thus, He led me far above,
And there, beneath a canopy of love,
Crosses of divers shape and size were seen,
Larger and smaller than my own had been.

And one there was, most beauteous to behold,
A little one, with jewels set in gold.
Ah! this, methought, I can with comfort wear,
For it will be an easy one to bear:

And so the little cross I quickly took;
But, all at once, my frame beneath it shook.
The sparkling jewels, fair were they to *see*,
But far too heavy was their *weight* for me.

" This may not be," I cried, and looked again,
To see if there was any here could ease my pain ;
But, one by one, I passed them slowly by,
Till on a lovely one I cast my eye.

Fair flowers around its sculptured form en-
    twined,
And grace and beauty seemed in it combined.
Wondering, I gazed ; and still I wondered more
To think so many should have passed it o'er.

But oh ! that form so beautiful to see
Soon made its hidden sorrows known to me ;
Thorns lay beneath those flowers and colours
    fair !
Sorrowing, I said : " This cross I may not bear."

And so it was with each and all around—
Not one to suit my *need* could there be found ;
Weeping, I laid each heavy burden down,
As my Guide gently said : " No cross, no
    crown ! "

At length, to Him I raised my saddened heart :
He knew its sorrows, bid its doubts depart.
" Be not afraid," He said, " but trust in me—
My perfect love shall now be shown to thee."

And then, with lightened eyes and willing feet,
Again I turned, my earthly cross to meet,
With forward footsteps, turning not aside,
For fear some hidden evil might betide ;

And there—in the prepared, appointed way,
Listening to hear, and ready to obey—
A cross I quickly found of plainest form,
With only words of love inscribed thereon.

With thankfulness I raised it from the rest,
And joyfully acknowledged it the best—
The only one of all the many there
That I could feel was good for me to bear.

And, while I thus my chosen one confessed,
I saw a heavenly brightness on it rest ;
And, as I bent, my burden to sustain,
I recognised my own old cross again.

But oh ! how different did it seem to be
Now I had learned its preciousness to see !
No longer could I unbelieving say,
Perhaps another is a better way.

Ah no ! henceforth my own desire shall be,
That He who knows me best should choose
        for me ;
And so, whate'er His love sees good to send,
I'll trust it's best, because He knows the end.

"For my thoughts are not your thoughts, saith the Lord."—
ISAIAH lv. 8

"For I know the thoughts that I think towards you—thoughts
of peace, and not of evil, to give you an expected end."—JER.
xxix. 11.

And when that happy time shall come, of endless peace and rest,
We shall look back upon our path, and say : It was the best.

The Meeting-Place.

WHERE the faded flower shall freshen,
  Freshen never more to fade ;
Where the shaded sky shall brighten,
  Brighten never more to shade ;
Where the sun-blaze never scorches ;
  Where the star-beams cease to chill ;
Where no tempest stirs the echoes
  Of the wood, or wave, or hill ;
Where the morn shall wake in gladness,
  And the moon the joy prolong ;
Where the daylight dies in fragrance
  'Mid the burst of holy song—
Brother, we shall meet and rest
'Mid the holy and the blest.

Where no shadow shall bewilder ;
  Where life's vain parade is o'er ;
Where the sleep of sin is broken,
  And the dreamer dreams no more ;
Where the bond is never severed—
  Partings, claspings, sobs, and moan,
Midnight waking, twilight weeping,
  Heavy noontide—all are done ;
Where the child has found its mother,
  Where the mother finds the child ;

Where dear families are gathered
That were scattered on the wild—
Brother, we shall meet and rest
'Mid the holy and the blest.

Where the hidden wound is healed;
Where the blighted light re-blooms;
Where the smitten heart the freshness
Of its buoyant youth resumes;
Where the love that here we lavish
On the withering leaves of time,
Shall have fadeless flowers to fix on,
In an ever spring-bright clime;
Where we find the joy of loving,
As we never loved before;
Loving on unchilled, unhindered,
Loving once and evermore—
Brother, we shall meet and rest
'Mid the holy and the blest.

Where a blasted world shall brighten
Underneath a bluer sphere,
And a softer, gentler sunshine
Shed its healing splendour here;
Where earth's barren vales shall blossom,
Putting on their robe of green,
And a purer, fairer Eden,
Be where only wastes have been;
Where a King, in kingly glory
Such as earth has never known,

Shall assume the righteous sceptre,
  Claim and wear the heavenly crown—
Brother, we shall meet and rest
'Mid the holy and the blest.

—⊷—

The Pilgrim.

STILL onward through this land of foes
  I pass in pilgrim guise;
I may not stop to seek repose
  Where cool the shadow lies;
I may not stoop amid the grass
  To pluck earth's fairest flowers,
Nor by her springing fountains pass
  The sultry noontide hours;

Yet flowers I wear upon my breast
  That no earth-garden knows—
White lilies of immortal peace,
  And love's deep-tinted rose;
And there the blue-eyed flowers of faith,
  And hope's bright buds of gold,
As lone I tread the upward path,
  In richest hues unfold.

I keep my armour ever on,
  For foes beset my way;
I watch lest, passing on alone,
  I fall a helpless prey.

No earthly love have I—I lean
  Upon no mortal breast;
But my Belovèd, though unseen,
  Walks near and gives me rest.

Afar, around, I often see,
  Throughout this desert wide,
His pilgrims pressing on like me—
  They often pass my side:
The kindly smile, the gentle word,
  For Jesus' sake I give;
But Love—O Thou alone adored!
  For Thee alone I live.

Painful and dark the pathway seems
  To distant earthly eyes;
They only see the hedging thorns
  On either side that rise;
They cannot know how soft between
  The flowers of love are strewn—
The sunny ways, the pastures green,
  Where Jesus leads His own;

They cannot see, as darkening clouds
  Behind the pilgrim close,
How far adown the western glade
  The golden glory flows;
They cannot hear 'mid earthly din
  The song to pilgrims known,
Still blending with the angels' hymn
  Around the wondrous throne.

So I, Thy bounteous token-flowers
  Still on my bosom wear;
While me, the fleeting love-winged hours
  To Thee still nearer bear:
So from my lips Thy song shall flow,
  My sweetest music be;
So on mine eyes the glory grow,
  Till all is lost in Thee.

———⋈———

holy Tears.

' YES, thou may'st weep, for Jesus shed
  Such tears as those thou sheddest now,
When, for the living or the dead,
  Sorrow lay heavy on His brow.

He sees thee weep, yet doth not blame
  The weakness of thy flesh and heart;
Thy human nature is the same ·
  As that in which He took a part.

He knows its weakness, for He felt
  The crushing power of pain and woe,
How body, soul, and spirit melt
  And faint beneath the stunning blow.

What if poor sinners count thy grief
  The sign of an unchastened will?
He who can give thy soul relief,
  Knows that thou art submissive still.

Turn thee to Him, to Him alone;
  For all that our poor lips can say
To soothe thee, broken-hearted one,
  Would fail to comfort thee to-day.

We will not speak to thee, but sit
  In prayerful silence by thy side:
Grief has its ebbs and flows; 'tis fit
  Our love should wait the ebbing tide.

Jesus himself will comfort thee,
  In His own time, in His own way;
And haply more than "two or three"
  Unite in prayer for thee to-day.

God our Strength.

MAN, in his weakness, needs a stronger stay
  Than fellow-men, the holiest and the best;
And yet we turn to them from day to day,
  As if in them our spirits could find rest.

Gently untwine our childish hands, that cling
  To such inadequate supports as these,
And shelter us beneath Thy heavenly wing,
  Till we have learned to walk alone with
    ease.

Help us, O Lord! with patient love to bear
  Each other's faults, to suffer with true meek-
      ness;
Help us each other's joys and griefs to share,
  But let us turn to Thee alone in weakness. •

Wholly Resigned.

CHRIST leads us through no darker rooms
  Than He went through before:
He that into God's kingdom comes,
  Must enter by this door.
Come, Lord, when Grace hath made me meet
  Thy blessed face to see,
For if Thy work on earth be sweet,
  What will Thy glory be!

Then I shall end my sad complaints,
  And weary, sinful days;
And join with the triumphant saints,
  That sing Jehovah's praise:
My knowledge of that life is small,
  The eye of faith is dim,
But 'tis enough that Christ knows all,
  And I shall be with Him.

"My Times are in Thy Hand."

PSALM xxxi. 15.

FATHER, I know that all my life
    Is portioned out for me,
And the changes that are sure to come,
    I do not fear to see ;
But I ask Thee for a present mind
    Intent on pleasing Thee.

I ask Thee for a thankful love,
    Through constant watching wise,
To meet the glad with joyful smiles,
    And to wipe the weeping eyes,
And a heart at leisure from itself,
    To soothe and sympathise.

I would not have the restless will
    That hurries to and fro,
Seeking for some great thing to do,
    Or secret thing to know ;
I would be dealt with as a child,
    And guided where to go.

Wherever in the world I am,
    In whatsoe'er estate,
I have a fellowship with hearts,
    To keep and cultivate,
And a work of holy love to do,
    For the Lord on whom I wait.

I ask Thee for the daily strength,
　　To none that ask denied ;
And a mind to blend with outward life,
　　While keeping at Thy side ;
Content to fill a little space,
　　If Thou be glorified.

And if some things I do not ask
　　In my cup of blessing be,
I would have my spirit filled the more
　　With grateful love to Thee—
More careful than to serve Thee much,
　　To please Thee perfectly.

There are briers besetting every path,
　　That call for patient care ;
There is a crook in every lot,
　　And a need for earnest prayer ;
But a lowly heart that leans on Thee
　　Is happy everywhere.

In a service that Thy love appoints,
　　There are no bonds for me,
For my secret heart is taught the truth
　　That makes Thy children " free ; "
And a life of self-renouncing love
　　Is a life of liberty.

—✦—

The Border=Lands.

FATHER, into Thy loving hands
    My feeble spirit I commit,
While wandering in these border-lands,
    Until Thy voice shall summon it.

Father, I would not dare to choose
    A longer life, an earlier death ;
I know not what my soul might lose
    By shortened or protracted breath.

These border-lands are calm and still,
    And solemn are their silent shades ;
And my heart welcomes them, until
    The light of life's long evening fades.

I heard them spoken of with dread,
    As fearful and unquiet places ;
Shades, where the living and the dead
    Look sadly in each others' faces :

But since Thy hand hath led me here,
    And I have seen the border-land—
Seen the dark river flowing near,
    Stood on its brink, as now I stand—

There has been nothing to alarm
    My trembling soul ; how could I fear
While thus encircled with Thine arm ?
    I never felt Thee half so near.

What should appal me in a place
   That brings me hourly nearer Thee?
When I may almost see Thy face—
   Surely 'tis here my soul would be.

They say the waves are dark and deep,
   That faith has perished in the river;
They speak of death with fear, and weep.
   Shall my soul perish?   Never! never!

I know that Thou wilt never leave
   The soul that trembles while it clings
To Thee : I know Thou wilt achieve
   Its passage on Thine outspread wings.

And since I first was brought so near
   The stream that flows to the Dead Sea,
I think that it has grown more clear
   And shallow than it used to be.

I cannot see the golden gate
   Unfolding yet to welcome me ;
I cannot yet anticipate
   The joy of heaven's jubilee ;

But I will calmly watch and pray
   Until I hear my Saviour's voice
Calling my happy soul away,
   To see His glory, and rejoice.

"All, all is known to Thee."

"When my spirit was overwhelmed within me, then Thou knewest my path."

My God, whose gracious pity I may claim,
Calling Thee Father—sweet, endearing name!
The sufferings of this weak and weary frame,
    All, all are known to Thee.

From human eye 'tis better to conceal
Much that I suffer, much I hourly feel;
But oh! the thought does tranquillise and heal—
    All, all is known to Thee.

Each secret conflict with indwelling sin,
Each sickening fear I ne'er the prize shall win,
Each pang from irritation, turmoil, din—
    All, all are known to Thee.

When in the morning unrefreshed I wake,
Or in the night but little sleep can take,
This brief appeal submissively I make—
    All, all is known to Thee.

Nay, all by Thee is ordered, chosen, planned—
Each drop that fills my daily cup; Thy hand
Prescribes for ills none else can understand.
    All, all is known to Thee.

The effectual means to cure what I deplore;
In me Thy longed-for likeness to restore;
Self to dethrone, never to govern more—
    All, all are known to Thee.

And this continued feebleness, this state
Which seems to unnerve and incapacitate,
Will work the cure my hopes and prayers
    await—
      That can I leave to Thee.

Nor will the bitter draught distasteful prove,
When I recall the SON of Thy dear love;
The cup Thou wouldst not for *our* sakes re-
    move—
      That cup He drank for *me.*

He drank it to the dregs—no drop remained
Of wrath for those whose cup of woe He
    drained;
Man ne'er can know what that sad cup con-
    tained—
      All, all is known to Thee.

And welcome, *precious*, can His Spirit make
My little drop of suffering for His sake.
Father! the cup I drink, the path I take,
      All, all is known to Thee.

— ⋈ —

Oh! for the happy Days gone by.

OH! for the happy days gone by,
    When love ran smooth and free;
Days when my spirit so enjoyed
    More than earth's liberty!

Oh ! for the times when on my heart
    Long prayer had never palled,
Times when the ready thought of God
    Would come when it was called!

Then when I knelt to meditate,
    Sweet thoughts came o'er my soul,
Countless and bright and beautiful,
    Beyond my own control.

Oh ! who hath locked those fountains up ?
    Those visions who hath staid ?
What sudden act hath thus transformed
    My sunshine into shade ?

This freezing heart, O Lord ! this will,
    Dry as the desert sand—
Good thoughts that will not come, bad thoughts
    That come without command—

A faith that seems not faith—a hope
    That cares not for its aim—
A love that none the hotter grows
    At Jesus' blessed name—

The weariness of prayer—the mist
    O'er conscience overspread—
The chill repugnance to frequent
    The feast of angels' bread :

If this drear change be Thine, O Lord !
    If it be Thy sweet will,

Spare not, but to the very brim
   The bitter chalice fill ;

But if it hath been sin of mine,
   Oh ! show that sin to me—
Not to get back the sweetness lost,
   But to make peace with Thee.

One thing alone, dear Lord, I dread—
   To have a secret spot
That separates my soul from Thee,
   And yet to know it not.

Oh ! when the tide of graces set
   So full upon my heart,
I know, dear Lord, how faithlessly
   I did my little part ;

I know how well my heart hath earned
   A chastisement like this,
In trifling many a grace away
   In self-complacent bliss.

But if this weariness hath come
   A present from on high,
Teach me to find the hidden wealth
   That in its depths may lie ;

So in this darkness I can learn
   To tremble and adore,
To sound my own vile nothingness,
   And thus to love Thee more ;—

To love Thee, and yet not to think
    That I can love so much ;
To have Thee with me, Lord ! all day,
    Yet not to feel Thy touch.

If I have served Thee, Lord ! for hire,
    Hire which Thy beauty showed,
Ah ! I can serve Thee now for naught,
    And only as my God.

Oh ! blessed be this darkness, then,
    This deep in which I lie ;
And blessed be all things that teach
    God's dread supremacy !

Lost Treasures.

LET us be patient, God has taken from us
    The earthly treasures upon which we leaned,
That from the fleeting things which lie around us
    Our clinging hearts should be for ever
        weaned.

They have passed from us—all our broad pos-
        sessions ;
    Ships, whose white sails flung wide past dis-
        tant shores ;
Lands, whose rich harvests smiled in the glad
        sunshine ;
    Silver and gold, and all our hoarded stores.

And, dearer far, the pleasant home where
    gathered
  Our loved and loving round the blazing
    hearth ;
Where honoured age on the soft cushions rested,
  And childhood played about in frolic mirth.

Where, underneath the softened light, bent
    kindly
  The mother's tender glance on daughters fair,
And he on whom all leant with fond confiding
  Rested contented from his daily care.

All shipwrecked in one common desolation !
  The garden-walks by other feet are trod ;
The clinging vines by other fingers tutored
  To fling their shadows o'er the grassy sod ;

While carking care and deep humiliation,
  In tears are mingled with their daily bread ;
And the rude blasts we never thought could
    reach us,
  Have spent there worst on each defenceless
    head.

Let us be cheerful ! The same sky o'erarches—
  Soft rain falls on the evil and the good ;
On narrow walls, and through our humbler
    dwelling
  God's glorious sunshine pours as rich a flood.

Faith, hope, and love, still in our hearts abiding,
　　May bear their precious fruits in us the same;
And to the couch of suffering we may carry,
　　If but the cup of water, in His name.

Let us be thankful, if in this affliction
　　No grave is opened for the loving heart;
And while we bend beneath our Father's chiding,
　　We yet can mourn "each family apart."

Shoulder to shoulder let us breast the torrent,
　　With not one cold reproach nor angry look;
There are some seasons, when the heart is
　　　　smitten,
　　It can no whisper of unkindness brook.

Our life is not in all these brief possessions;
　　Our home is not in any pleasant spot:
Pilgrims and strangers, we must journey on-
　　　　ward,
　　Contented with the portion of our lot.

These earthly walls must shortly be dismantled,
　　These earthly tents be struck by angel hands;
But to be built up on a sure foundation,
　　There, where our Father's mansion ever
　　　　stands.

There shall we meet, parent and child, and
　　　　dearer,
　　That earthly love which makes half heaven
　　　　of home;

There shall we find our treasures all awaiting,
  Where change and death and parting never
    come.

—*—

Sunday.

"I was in the spirit on the Lord's day."—REV. i. 10.

AFTER long days of storms and showers,
Of sighing winds, and dripping bowers,
How sweet at morn to ope our eyes
On newly "swept and garnished" skies!—

To miss the clouds, and driving rain,
And see that all is bright again—
So bright we cannot choose but say,
Is this the world of yesterday?

Even so, methinks, the Sunday brings
A change o'er all familiar things;
A change—we know not whence it came—
They are, and they are not, the same.

There is a spell within, around,
On eye and ear, on sight and sound,
And, loth or willing, they and we
Must own this day a mystery.

Sure all things wear a heavenly dress,
That sanctifies their loveliness,
Types of that endless resting-day,
When "we shall all be changed" as they.

To-day our peaceful, ordered home
Foreshadoweth mansions yet to come,
We foretaste, in domestic love,
The faultless charities above.

And as at yester eventide
Our tasks and toys were laid aside,
Lo! here our training for the day
When we shall lay them down for aye.

But not alone for musings deep,
Meek souls their "day of days" will keep;
Yet other glorious things than these
The Christian in his Sabbath sees.

His eyes, by faith, his Lord behold;
How on the week's first day of old
From Hell He rose, on Death He trod,
Was seen of men, and went to God.

And as we fondly pause to look
Where, in some daily-handled book,
Approval's well-known tokens stand,
Traced by some dear and thoughtful hand,

Even so there shines one day in seven
Bright with the special mark of Heaven,
That we with love and praise may dwell
On Him who loveth us so well;

Whether in meditative walk,
Alone with God and Heaven we talk,

Catching the simple chime that calls
Our feet to some old church's walls ;

Or passed within the church's door,
Where poor are rich, and rich are poor,
We say the prayers, and hear the word,
Which there our fathers said and heard ;

Or represent in solemn wise
Our all-prevailing sacrifice,
Feeding in joint communion high
The life of faith that cannot die.

And surely in a world like this,
So rife with woe, so scant of bliss—
Where fondest hopes are oftenest crossed,
And fondest hopes are severed most—

'Tis something that we kneel and pray
With loved ones near and far away ;
One God, one faith, one hope, one care,
One form of words, one hour of prayer.

'Tis just ; yet pause, till ear and heart,
In one brief silence, ere we part,
Somewhat of that high strain have caught—
" The peace of God which passeth thought."

Then turn we to our earthly homes,
Not doubting but that Jesus comes,
Breathing His peace on hall and hut,
At evening, when the doors are shut ;

Then speeds us on our work-day way,
And hallows every common day;
Without *Him* Sunday's self were dim,
But all are bright, *if spent with Him.*

———✶———

One by One.

ONE by one the sands are flowing,
  One by one the moments fall;
Some are coming, some are going—
  Do not strive to grasp them all.

One by one thy duties wait thee,
  Let thy whole strength go to each;
Let no future dreams elate thee—
  Learn thou first what those can teach.

One by one (bright gifts from heaven),
  Joys are sent thee here below;
Take them readily, when given—
  Ready, too, to let them go.

One by one thy griefs shall meet thee,
  Do not fear an armèd band;
One will fade while others greet thee—
  Shadows passing through the land.

Do not look at life's long sorrow,
  See how small each moment's pain;
God will help thee for to-morrow—
  Every day begin again.

Every hour that fleets so slowly,
   Has its task to do or bear ;
Luminous the crown, and holy,
   If thou set each gem with care.

Do not linger with regretting,
   Or for passion's hour despond ;
Nor, the daily toil forgetting,
   Look too eagerly beyond.

Hours are golden links, God's token,
   Reaching heaven ; but one by one
Take them, lest the chain be broken
   Ere the pilgrimage be done.

—✠—

Mary's Choice.

JESUS, engrave it on my heart,
That Thou the one thing needful art ;
I could from all things parted be,
But never, never, Lord, from Thee.

Needful is Thy most precious blood,
Needful is Thy correcting rod,
Needful is Thy indulgent care,
Needful Thy all-prevailing prayer.

Needful Thy presence, dearest Lord,
True peace and comfort to afford :
Needful Thy promise to impart
Fresh life and vigour to my heart,

Needful art Thou to be my stay
Through all life's dark and thorny way;
Nor less in death Thou'lt needful be,
To bring my spirit home to Thee.

Then, needful still, my God, my King,
Thy name eternally I'll sing:
Glory and praise be ever His—
The "one thing needful" Jesus is.

— ⋈ —

"Nearer Home."

ONE sweetly solemn thought
  Comes to me o'er and o'er:
I'm nearer home to-day
  Than I ever have been before;

Nearer my Father's house,
  Where the many mansions be;
Nearer the great white throne,
  Nearer the jasper sea;

Nearer the bound of life,
  Where we lay our burdens down;
Nearer leaving the cross,
  Nearer wearing the crown.

But lying darkly between,
  Winding down through the night,
Is the dim and unknown stream
  That leads at last to the light.

Closer, closer my steps
   Come to the dark abysm ;
Closer, death to my lips
  ` Presses the awful chrism.

Saviour ! perfect my trust,
   Strengthen the might of my faith ;
Let me feel as I would when I stand
   On the rock of the shore of death—

Feel as I would when my feet
   Are slipping over the brink ;
For it may be I'm nearer home,
   Nearer now than I think.

—>•<—

Oh! to be ready.

OH ! to be ready when death shall come !
Oh ! to be ready to hasten home !
No earthward clinging, no lingering gaze,
No strife at parting, no sore amaze ;
No chains to sever that earth hath twined,
No spell to loosen that love would bind ;

No flitting shadows to dim the light
Of the angel-pinions winged for flight ;
No cloud-like phantoms to fling a gloom
'Twixt heaven's bright portals and earth's dark
    tomb ;
But sweetly, gently, to pass away
From the world's dim twilight into day.

C

To list the music of angel lyres,
To catch the rapture of seraph fires;
To lean in trust on the risen One,
Till borne away to a fadeless throne.
Oh! to be ready when death shall come!
Oh! to be ready to hasten home!

———>+<———

𝕮𝖍𝖊 𝕭𝖗𝖎𝖉𝖊𝖌𝖗𝖔𝖔𝖒'𝖘 𝕯𝖔𝖛𝖊.

" O my dove! in the clefts of the rock, in the secret of the
stairs."—CANT. ii. 14.

"My dove!" The Bridegroom speaks.
    To whom?
Whom, think'st thou, meaneth He?
Say, O my soul! canst thou presume
    He thus addresseth thee?
Yes, 'tis the Bridegroom's voice of love,
Calling thee, O my soul! His dove!

The dove is gentle, mild, and meek;
    Deserve I, then, the name?
I look within in vain to seek
    Aught which can give a claim:
Yet, made so by redeeming love,
My soul, thou art the Bridegroom's dove!

Methinks, my soul, that thou may'st see,
    In this endearing word,
Reasons why Jesus likens thee
    To this defenceless bird—

Reasons which show the Bridegroom's love
To His poor helpless, timid dove!

The dove, of all the feathered tribe,
   Doth least of power possess;
My soul, what better can describe
   Thine utter helplessness?
Yet courage take! the Bridegroom's love
Will keep, defend, protect His dove!

The dove hath neither claw nor sting,
   Nor weapon for the fight;
She owes her safety to her wing,
   Her victory to flight.
A shelter hath the Bridegroom's love
Provided for His helpless dove!

The hawk comes on, in eager chase—
   The dove will not resist;
In flying to her hiding-place
   Her safety doth consist.
The Bridegroom opes His arms of love,
And in them folds His panting dove!

Nothing the dove can now molest;
   Safe from the fowler's snare,
The Bridegroom's bosom is her nest—
   Nothing can harm her there:
Encircled by the arms of love,
Almighty power protects the dove!

As the poor dove, before the hawk,
    Quick to her refuge flies,
So need I, in my daily walk,
    The wing which faith supplies,
To bear me where the Bridegroom's love
Places beyond all harm His dove !

My soul, of native power bereft,
    To Calvary repairs :
Immanuel is the *rocky cleft,*
    " *The secret of the stairs !* "
Since placed *there* by the Bridegroom's love,
What evil can befall His dove ?

Though Sinai's thunder round her roars,
    Though Ebal's lightnings flash,
Though heaven a fiery torrent pours,
    And riven mountains crash—
Through all, the " still, small voice " of love
Whispers : " Be not afraid, my dove ! "

What though the heavens away may pass,
    With fervent heat dissolve ;
And round the sun this earthly mass
    No longer shall revolve !
Behold a miracle of love !
The lion quakes, but not the dove !

My soul, now hid within a rock,
    (The " Rock of Ages " called)

Amid the universal shock
  Is fearless, unappalled.
A cleft therein, prepared by love,
In safety hides the Bridegroom's dove!

O happy dove! thus weak, thus safe!
  Do I resemble her?
Then to my soul, O Lord! vouchsafe
  A *dove-like* character!
Pure, harmless, gentle, full of love,
Make me in spirit, Lord, a dove!

O Thou, who on the Bridegroom's head
  Didst as a dove come down,
Within my soul Thy graces shed,
  Establish there Thy throne;
There shed abroad a Saviour's love,
Thou holy, pure, and heavenly Dove!

S. R. M.

God, my Exceeding Joy.

PSALM xliii. 4.

EARLY my spirit turned
  From earthly things away,
And agonised and yearned
  For the eternal day;
Dimly I saw, when but a boy,
  God, my exceeding joy.

In days of fiercer flame,
  When passion urged me on,
'Twas only bliss in name—
  The pleasure soon was gone.
Compared with Thee, how all things cloy,
  God, my exceeding joy !

At length the moment came—
  Jesus made known His love ;
High shot the kindling flame
  To glories all above.
Now all my powers one theme employ,
  God, my exceeding joy.

Shadows came on apace ;
  Tears were a pensive shower ;
I cried for timely grace
  To save me from the hour ;
Thou gavest peace without alloy,
  God, my exceeding joy.

One trial yet awaits,
  Gigantic at the close ;
All that my spirit hates
  May then my peace oppose :
But God shall this last foe destroy,
  God, my exceeding joy.

God's Support and Guidance.

TRANSLATED FROM THE GERMAN.

FORSAKE me not, my God,
  Thou God of my salvation !
Give me Thy light, to be
  My sure illumination.
My soul to folly turns,
  Seeking she knows not what ;
Oh ! lead her to Thyself—
  My God, forsake me not !

Forsake me not, my God !
  Take not Thy Spirit from me :
And suffer not the might
  Of sin to overcome me.
A father pitieth
  The children he begot ; ·
My Father, pity me—
  My God, forsake me not.

Forsake me not, my God,
  Thou God of life and power,
Enliven, strengthen me
  In every evil hour ;
And when the sinful fire
  Within my heart is hot,
Be not thou far from me—
  My God, forsake me not !

Forsake me not, my God !
  Uphold me in my going,
That evermore I may
  Please Thee in all well-doing :
And that Thy will, O Lord !
  May never be forgot,
In all my works and ways—
  My God, forsake me not !

Forsake me not, my God !
  I would be Thine for ever !
Confirm me mightily
  In every right endeavour :
And when my hour is come,
  Cleansed from all stain and spot
Of sin, receive my soul —
  My God, forsake me not !

I Am.

"God calls Himself I AM, leaving a blank which each soul
may fill up with that which is most precious to himself."

THOU bidd'st us call, and giv'st us many a
      name,
  That Thou may'st hear and answer every
      cry.
But—for the wants of all are not the same—
  Another name Thy wondrous love did try ;
To Moses first thou gav'st it, and he knew
Its worth, and taught us how to prize it, too—

I AM—let every sinner kneel, and thank
The Lord, and with his wants fill up the blank.
Thy very wounds do say, each drop they bleed,
    " I AM thy need."

Oh ! I am weary of this life,
   Of all its vanity and care ;
Where can I hide me from its strife,
   From all its noises—where ?
My spirit sinks beneath the load,
I pant to reach a safe abode.
When shall I find a sweet release ?
Remains there yet a lasting peace,
A calm for my long storm-tossed breast ?
    " I AM thy rest."

Oh ! I am full of grievous sin,
   I can do naught that's right.
O God ! how base my soul is in
   Thy pure and holy sight !
Thy perfect laws I daily, hourly break,
And will not yield my will for Thy sweet sake :
Still in my soul do burn wicked desires,
And my heart's altar bears unhallowed fires ;
I can do naught but all these things confess,
    " I AM thy righteousness."

But, Lord, I am so weak, so weak,
   I cannot stand before Thy face ;
Thy praises I can hardly speak,
   Hardly stretch forth my hands for grace ;

The way seems long, the burden who can bear,
Lord, must I sink beneath the load of care?
Thus is it now; what shall it be at length?
    "I AM thy strength."

Lord, I must die: e'en now the wing
   Of Thy dread angel hovereth nigh;
I know the message he doth bring—
   "Soul, thou hast sinned, and thou must die."
All nature feels and owns the just decree;
And is this all that is in store for me—
Ashes to ashes, dust to kindred dust,
No hope, no light? Surely my spirit must
Sink in despair ere nature's last, fierce strife!
    "I AM thy life."

Oh! wonderful Thou art!
   Too wonderful for me is such great love,
Shining in such a heart
   Like sunbeams from above.
How rich am I! yea, all things I possess—
Peace, joy, life, strength, and perfect righteous-
    ness.
Jehovah shows Himself, and gives to me
All my desire. Look, trembling soul! and see
On what a treasury thy want may call!—
    "I AM thine all in all."

A Little While.

BEYOND the smiling and the weeping
        I shall be soon ;
Beyond the waking and the sleeping,
Beyond the sowing and the reaping,
        I shall be soon.
            Love, rest, and home !
                Sweet hope !
        Lord, tarry not, but come.

Beyond the blooming and the fading
        I shall be soon ;
Beyond the shining and the shading,
Beyond the hoping and the dreading,
        I shall be soon.
            Love, rest, and home !·
                Sweet hope !
        Lord, tarry not, but come.

Beyond the rising and the setting
        I shall be soon ;
Beyond the calming and the fretting,
Beyond remembering and forgetting,
        I shall be soon.
            Love, rest, and home !
                Sweet hope !
        Lord, tarry not, but come,

Beyond the gathering and the strewing
I shall be soon;
Beyond the ebbing and the flowing,
Beyond the coming and the going,
I shall be soon.
Love, rest, and home!
Sweet hope!
Lord, tarry not, but come.

Beyond the parting and the meeting
I shall be soon;
Beyond the farewell and the greeting,
Beyond this pulse's fever beating,
I shall be soon.
Love, rest, and home!
Sweet hope!
Lord, tarry not, but come.

Beyond the frost-chain and the fever
I shall be soon;
Beyond the rock-waste and the river,
Beyond the ever and the never,
I shall be soon.
Love, rest, and home!
Sweet hope!
Lord, tarry not, but come,

Hinder me Not.

HINDER me not! the path is long and weary,
    I may not pause nor tarry by the way ;
Night cometh, when no man may journey on-
    ward,
    For we must walk as children of the day.

I know the city lieth fair behind me,
    The very brightest gem that studs the plain ;
But thick and fast the lurid clouds are rising,
    Which soon shall scatter into fiery rain.

I must press on until I reach my Zoar,
    And there find refuge from the fearful blast ;
In Thy cleft side, O smitten Saviour ! hide me,
    Till the calamity be overpast.

Ye cannot tempt me back with pomp or plea-
    sure,
    All, in my eager grasp, have turned to dust ;
The shield of love around my hearth is broken,
    How shall I place on man's frail life my trust ?

But my heart lingers when I pass the dwellings
    Where children play about the open door,
And pleasant voices waken up the echoes
    From silent lips of those I see no more :

For through their chambers swept the solemn
    warning,
  Arise ! depart ! for this is not your rest ;
They folded their pale hands and sought the
    presence—
  I only bore the arrow in my breast.

But there is balm in Gilead, and a Healer
  Whose sovereign power can cure our every ill ;
And to the soul, more wildly tempest-tossing
  Than ever Galilee, say : " Peace ! be still ! "

Who, showing His own name thereon engraven,
  With bleeding hands will draw the dart again,
And whisper : " Should the true disciple
    murmur
  To taste the cup his Master's lip could
    drain ? "

And then lead on, until we reach the river
  Which all must cross, and some must cross
    alone.
Oh ! ye who in the land of peace are wearied,
  How shall ye breast the Jordan's swelling
    moan ?

I know not if the wave shall rage or slumber
  When I shall stand upon the nearer shore ;
But One whose form the Son of God resembleth,
  Will cross with me, and I shall ask no more.

O weary heads ! rest on your Saviour's bosom.
   O weary feet ! press on the path He trod.
O weary souls ! your rest shall be remaining,
   When ye have gained the city of your God.

O glorious city ! jasper built, and shining
   With God's own glory in effulgent light,
Wherein no manner of defilement cometh,
   Nor any shadow flung from passing night :

There shall ye pluck fruits from that tree
    immortal,
   And be like gods, but find no curse therein ;
There shall ye slake your thirst in that full
    fountain
   Whose distant streams suffice to cleanse your
    sin ;

There shall ye find your dead in Christ arisen,
   And learn from them to sing the angels' song ;
Well may ye echo from earth's waiting prison
   The martyrs' cry : " How long, O Lord ! how
    long ! "

—+—

"I Cling to Thee."

O HOLY SAVIOUR ! Friend unseen !
Since on Thine arm thou bidd'st me lean,
Help me throughout life's varying scene :
   By faith I cling to Thee.

Blest with this fellowship divine,
Take what Thou wilt, I'll ne'er repine :
E'en as the branches to the vine,
    My soul would cling to Thee.

Far from her home, fatigued, oppressed,
Here has she found her place of rest,
An exile still, yet not unblessed,
    While she can cling to Thee.

What though the world deceitful prove,
And earthly friends and joys remove ;
With patient, uncomplaining love,
    Still would I cling to Thee.

Though faith and hope may long be tried,
I ask not, need not aught beside.
How safe, how calm, how satisfied,
    The soul that clings to Thee !

They fear not Satan, nor the grave ;
They feel Thee near, and strong to save ;
Nor dread to cross e'en Jordan's wave,
    Because they cling to Thee !

Blest is my lot : whate'er befall,
What can disturb me—who appal ?
While, as my strength, my rock, my all,
    Saviour ! I cling to Thee.

"Alone, yet not Alone."

When no kind earthly friend is near,
With gentle words my heart to cheer,
Still am I with my Saviour dear:
　　"Alone, yet not alone."

Though no loved forms my path attend,
With tender looks o'er me to bend,
Yet am I with my unseen Friend:
　　"Alone, yet not alone."

When sorely racked with pain and grief,
Here I can find a sure relief;
And I rejoice in the belief:
　　"Alone, yet not alone."

'Tis on His strength that I rely,
And doubts and fears at once defy,
So happy, so content am I,
　　"Alone, yet not alone."

E'en when with friends my lot is cast,
And words of love are flowing fast,
Still am I, when those hours are past,
　　"Alone, yet not alone."

If all my earthly friends remove,
My fondest wishes empty prove,
Still am I, with my Saviour's love,
　　"Alone, yet not alone."

D

Whate'er may now to me betide,
I have a place wherein to hide
By faith ; 'tis e'en at His blest side :
    "Alone, yet not alone."

———→+←———

The School of Suffering.

SAVIOUR ! beneath Thy yoke
    My wayward heart doth pine ;
All unaccustomed to the stroke
    Of love divine :
Thy chastisements, my God, are hard to bear,
Thy cross is heavy for frail flesh to wear.

"Perishing child of clay !
    Thy sighing I have heard ;
Long have I marked thy evil way,
    How thou hast erred !
Yet fear not : by my own most holy name,
I will shed healing through thy sin-sick frame."

Praise to Thee, gracious Lord !
    I fain would be at rest ;
Oh ! now fulfil Thy faithful word,
    And make me blest ;
My soul would lay her heavy burden down,
And take with joyfulness the promised crown.

"Stay, thou short-sighted child !
    There is much first to do :

Thy heart, so long by sin defiled,
    I must renew !
Thy will must here be taught to bend to mine,
Or the sweet peace of heaven can ne'er be
    thine."

    Yea, Lord, but Thou canst soon
      Perfect Thy work in me,
    Till, like the pure, calm summer noon,
      I shine by Thee—
A moment shine, that all Thy power may trace,
Then pass in stillness to my heavenly place.

    "Ah, coward soul ! confess
      Thou shrinkest from my cure,
    Thou tremblest at the sharp distress
      Thou must endure—
The foes on every hand for war arrayed,
The thorny path in tribulation laid ;

    " The process slow of years,
      The discipline of life ;
Of outward woes and secret tears,
      Sickness and strife ;
Thine idols taken from thee one by one,
Till thou canst dare to live with me alone.

    "Some gentle souls there are
      Who yield unto my love,
Who, ripening fast beneath my care,
      I soon remove ;

But thou stiff-necked art, and hard to rule ;
Thou must stay longer in affliction's school."

> My Maker and my King !
>   Is this Thy love to me ?
> Oh ! that I had the lightning's wing,
>   From earth to flee !
> How can I bear the heavy weight of woes
> Thine indignation on the creature throws ?

> " Thou canst not, O my child !
>   So hear my voice again :
> I will bear all thy anguish wild,
>   Thy grief, thy pain ;
> My arm shall be around thee, day by day ;
> My smile shall cheer thee on thy heavenward
>   way.

> " In sickness, I will be
>   Watching beside thy bed ;
> In sorrow thou shalt lean on me
>   Thy aching head ;
> In every struggle thou shalt conqueror prove,
> Nor death itself shall sever from my love."

> O grace beyond compare !
>   O love most high and pure !
> Saviour, begin, no longer spare,
>   I can endure ;
> Only vouchsafe Thy grace, that I may live
> Unto Thy glory, who canst so forgive.

The Pilgrim's Wants.

I WANT that adorning divine,
 Thou, only, my God, canst bestow;
I want in those beautiful garments to shine,
 Which distinguish Thy household below.
         Col. iii. 12–17.

I want, oh! I want to attain
 Some likeness, my Saviour, to Thee;
That longed-for resemblance once more to
  regain,
 Thy comeliness put upon me.
         1 John iii. 2, 3.

I want to be marked for Thy own;
 Thy seal on my forehead to wear;
To receive that "new name" on the mystic
  white stone,
 Which only Thyself canst declare.
         Rev. ii. 17.

I want, every moment, to feel
 That the Spirit does dwell in my heart;
That His power is present to cleanse and to
  heal,
 And newness of life to impart.
         Rom. viii. 11–16.

I want so in Thee to abide,
 As to bring forth some fruit to Thy praise;

The branch that Thou prunest, though feeble
    and dried,
   May languish, but never decays.
                    John xv. 2–5.

I want Thine own hand to unbind
   Each tie to terrestrial things,
Too tenderly cherished, too closely entwined,
   Where my heart too tenaciously clings.
                    1 John ii. 15.

I want, by my aspect serene,
   My actions and words, to declare
That my treasure is placed in a country unseen,
   That my heart and affections are there.
                    Matt. vi. 19–21.

I want, as a traveller, to haste
   Straight onward, nor pause on my way;
No forethought or anxious contrivance to waste
   On my tent, only pitched for a day.
                    Heb. xiii. 5, 6.

I want (and this sums up my prayer)
   To glorify Thee till I die;
Then calmly to yield up my soul to Thy care,
   And breathe out in prayer my last sigh.
                    Phil. iii. 8, 9.

Heaven.

OH! heaven is nearer than mortals think,
　　When they look, with a trembling dread,
At the misty future that stretches on
　　From the silent home of the dead.

'Tis no lone isle on a boundless main,
　　No brilliant but distant shore,
Where the lovely ones who are called away
　　Must go to return no more.

No—heaven is near us; the mighty veil
　　Of mortality blinds the eye,
That we cannot see the angel bands
　　On the shore of eternity.

The eye that shuts in a dying hour
　　Will open the next in bliss;
The welcome will sound in the heavenly world
　　Ere the farewell is hushed in this.

We pass from the clasp of mourning friends,
　　To the arms of the loved and lost;
And those smiling faces will greet us there,
　　Which on earth we have valued most.

Yet oft, in the hours of holy thought,
　　To the thirsting soul is given
That power to pierce through the mist of sense,
　　To the beauteous scenes of heaven.

Then very near seem its pearly gates,
   And sweetly its harpings fall;
Till the soul is restless to soar away,
   And longs for the angel's call.

I know, when the silver cord is loosed,
   When the veil is rent away,
Not long and dark shall the passage be,
   To the realms of endless day.

———+———

A Voice From Heaven.

I SHINE in the light of God,
   His image stamps my brow;
Through the shadows of death my feet have trod,
   And I reign in glory now.
No breaking heart is here,
   No keen and thrilling pain,
No wasted cheek, where the burning tear
   Hath rolled and left its stain.

I have found the joys of heaven;
   I am one of the angel band;
To my head a crown is given,
   And a harp is in my hand;
I have learned the song they sing,
   Whom Jesus hath made free,
And the glorious walls of heaven still ring
   With my new-born melody.

No sin, no grief, no pain—
   Safe in my happy home :
My fears all fled, my doubts all slain,
   My hour of triumph come.
O friends of my mortal years !
   The trusted and the true,
You're walking still the vale of tears,
   But I wait to welcome you.

Do I forget ?   Oh, no !
   For memory's golden chain
Shall bind my heart to the hearts below
   Till they meet and touch again ;
Each link is strong and bright,
   While love's electric flame
Flows freely down, like a river of light,
   To the world from whence I came.

Do you mourn when another star
   Shines out from the glorious sky ?
Do you weep when the voice of war
   And the rage of conflict die ?
Why then should your tears roll down,
   Or your heart be sorely riven,
For another gem in the Saviour's crown,
   And another soul in heaven ?

Supplication.

LORD, hear my prayer!
Turn not Thine ear from my distress,
But with Thy loving mercy bless,
　　Lest I despair.

　Be gracious, Lord;
My soul is oft opprest and weak;
Oh! aid me when I comfort seek
　　In Thy blest Word.

　My footsteps stray;
I wander often from the road
That leads to peace and Thee, my God:
　　Teach Thou the way.

　Oh! make me pure;
Clothe Thou my soul in spotless white,
That my acceptance in Thy sight,
　　Be always sure.

Let me be one
Of all the sinless company,
That round Thy throne hosannahs sing,
　　Through Christ, Thy Son.

　Thy will be done
On earth, as by each holy one,
Thy own redeemed, who near Thy throne,
　　Bow down the knee!

　　　　　　　　R——N.

Evening Prayer.

FATHER of mercy! at the close of day,
My work and duties done, to Thee I pray
  Before I sleep;
With claspèd hands I humbly bow my head,
And ask Thee, Lord, ere I retire to bed,
  My soul to keep.

The sins and failings of the day now past,
The shadows on my soul that they have cast,
  Do thou forgive.
Oh! purge my life from every taint of sin,
That I within Thy courts may enter in,
  With Thee to live.

Whatever sorrow I this day have known,
I spread it now, O Lord! before Thy throne—
  Oh! succour send:
I would beneath Thy chastening hand be still,
And meekly bow before Thy sovereign will,
  Unto the end.

And now, with folded hand upon my breast,
At peace with Thee, I lay me down to rest
  Upon my bed;
May angels guard me through the darksome
  night,
From troubled dreams, until the morning light
  Its beams shall shed.

       R——N.

The Wandering Heart.

ALAS! for the wild wandering heart,
   And its changing idol guests!
It has roamed away to the world's far ends,
   At the vagrant wind's behests,
More fleet in its course than the flying dart—
Alas! for the wandering heart.

Go, bind it with Memory's holiest spells,
   But it recks not the things of old;
Go, chain it in Gratitude's surest cells,
   With fetters more precious than gold;
Yet ever, oh! ever, it will depart—
Alas! for the wandering heart.

Is it gone up to listen at heaven's gate
   To Gabriel's lyre of praise?
And to catch the deep chanting where seraphs
      wait,
   As a lesson for its mortal rays?
Oh, no! for it loves from such lessons to part—
Alas! for the wandering heart.

It loves on a worthless and treacherous world
   To bestow its high desires;
And the lamp which it ought to be lighting in
      heaven
   It kindles at idol fires;
Full seldom it turns to its guiding chart—
Alas! for the wandering heart.

It needs to be steeped in the briny wave
  Of affliction's billowy sea,
And salt tears must water its way to the grave,
  Ere it will from these vanities flee ;
It must ever be feeling the chastening smart—
Alas ! for the wandering heart.

My Father ! my Father ! this heart would be
     Thine :
Restore from its wanderings ;
Oh ! visit and nourish Thy wilderness-vine,
  Though it be from the bitter springs ;
Till the years of its pruning in time shall be
     o'er
And its shoots in eternity wander no more !

"Return thee to thy Rest."

RETURN, return thee to thine only rest,
  Lone pilgrim of the world !
  Far erring from the fold,
By the dark night and risen storms distressed ;
List ! weary lamb, the Shepherd's anxious voice,
And once again within His arms rejoice.

Return, return ! thy fair white fleece is soiled
  And by sharp briers rent,
  Thy little strength is spent ;
Yet He will pity thee, thou torn and spoiled.

There ! thou art cradled on His tender breast ;
Now never more, sweet lamb, forsake that rest.

Return, return, my soul ! be like this lamb.
 Yet can it, can it be,
 That Thou shouldst pardon me,
Thou injured Love ! all ingrate as I am,
Once again weary of earth's trifling things,
False as the desert's far and shining springs ?

Return, return to thy forsaken Friend,
 So long despised, forgot,
That now, thou wandering heart, 'twere just
 If He should " know thee not ; "
Yet on, press on, towards the mercy-seat,
And if thou perish, perish at His feet.

Return, return ! for He is near the dwelling,
 And not into the air
 Need rise the sighs of prayer.
Into His ear thou'rt all thy sorrows telling ;
Thou need'st not speak to Him through spaces
  wide,
For He is near thee, even at thy side.

" Him have I pierced "—oh ! I come, I come !
 My heart is broken, Lord :
 It needs nor voice nor word ;
One only look brought Peter back of yore ;
How bitterly I weep as then he wept !
Henceforth, oh ! keep me, and I shall be kept.

Near Jesus.

I WANT to live near Jesus,
   And never go astray ;
To feel that I am growing
   More like Him every day ;
That I am always laying
   My treasure up above,
And gaining more the spirit
   Of His gentleness and love.

I want such steadfast purpose
   My mission to fulfil,
That it may be my meat and drink
   To do my Father's will,
To follow in His footsteps,
   Who never turned aside
From the path that leads to heaven,
   Though often sorely tried.

Oh ! that in His humility
   My spirit may be clad !
That I may have the patience
   My suffering Saviour had !
A heart more disengaged
   From earth and earthly things,
Which through life's varied trials
   To Jesus simply clings !

Oh ! I shall live near Jesus,
   And never go astray,

And évery sin-defiling stain
   Shall soon be washed away ;
And I'll bear my Master's image
   When I see Him face to face,
Then earth shall lose the power
   Its brightness to deface.

—•—

Who is my Brother?

MUST I my brother keep,
   And share his pains and toil,
And weep with those that weep,
   And smile with those that smile ;
And act to each a brother's part,
   And feel his sorrows in my heart ?

Must I his burden bear
   As though it were my own,
And do as I would care
   Should to myself be done ;
And faithful to his interests prove,
   And as myself my neighbour love ?

Must I reprove his sin,
   Must I partake his grief,
And kindly enter in
   And minister relief—
The naked clothe, the hungry feed,
   And love him, not in word but deed ?

Then, Jesus, at Thy feet
   A student let me be,
And learn, as it is meet,
   My duty, Lord, of Thee;
For Thou didst come on mercy's plan,
And all Thy life was love to man.

Oh! make me as Thou art;
   Thy Spirit, Lord, bestow—
The kind and gentle heart,
   That feels another's woe;
That thus I may be like my Head,
And in my Saviour's footsteps tread.

———*———

Pilgrim of Earth.

PILGRIM of earth, who art journeying to
   heaven!
   Heir of eternal life! child of the day!
Cared for, watched over, beloved and forgiven—
   Art thou discouraged because of the way?

·Cared for, watched over, though often thou
   seemest
   Justly forsaken, nor counted a child;
Loved and forgiven, though rightly thou
   deemest
   Thyself all unlovely, impure, and defiled.

E

Weary and thirsty, no water-brook near thee,
    Press on, nor faint at the length of the
        way;
The God of thy life will assuredly hear thee—
    He will provide thee strength for the day.

Break through the brambles and briers that
        obstruct thee,
    Dread not the gloom and the blackness of
        night;
Lean on the Hand that will safely conduct
        thee,
    Trust to His eye to whom darkness is light.

Be trustful, be steadfast, whatever betide thee;
    Only one thing do thou ask of the Lord—
Grace to go forward wherever He guide thee,
    Simply believing the truth of His word.

Still on thy spirit deep anguish is pressing,
    Not for the yoke that His wisdom bestows:
A heavier burden thy soul is distressing—
    A heart that is slow in His love to repose;

Earthliness, coldness, unthankful behaviour;—
    Ah! thou mayest sorrow, but do not despair;
Even this grief thou mayest bring to thy
        Saviour,
    Cast upon Him e'en this burden and care!

Bring all thy hardness—His power can sub-
    due it;
  How full is the promise! the blessing how
    free!
"Whatsoever ye ask, in my name, I will do it:
  Abide in my love, and be joyful in me."

—⚬—

"What is this that He saith: A little while?"

JOHN xvi. 18.

OH! for the peace which floweth as a river,
  Making life's desert places bloom and smile!
Oh! for a faith to grasp heaven's bright "for
    ever,"
  Amid the shadows of earth's "little while!"

"A little while" for patient vigil-keeping,
  To face the storm, to wrestle with the strong;
"A little while" to sow the seed with weeping,
  Then bind the sheaves and sing the harvest-
    song.

"A little while" to wear the robe of sadness,
  To toil with weary step through erring ways;
Then to pour forth the fragrant oil of gladness,
  And clasp the girdle of the robe of praise.

"A little while" 'mid shadow and illusion
    To strive by faith Love's mysteries to spell;
Then reap each dark enigma's clear solution,
    Then hail Light's verdict—"He doth all
        things well."

"A little while" the earthen pitcher taking
    To wayside brooks from far-off fountains fed;
Then the parched lip its thirst for ever slaking
    Beside the fulness of the Fountain-Head.

"A little while" to keep the oil from failing;
    "A little while" Faith's flickering lamp to
        trim,
And then the Bridegroom's coming footstep
        hailing,
    To haste to meet Him with the bridal hymn.

And He who is at once both Gift and Giver,
    The future glory, and the present smile,
With the bright promise of the glad "for ever,"
    Will light the shadows of the "little while."

In Heaven.

"Their angels do always behold the face of my Father."

SILENCE filled the courts of heaven,
Hushed were seraphs' harp and tone,
When a little new-born seraph
Knelt before the Eternal Throne ;
While its soft white hands were lifted,
Clasped, as if in earnest prayer,
And its voice, in dove-like murmurs,
Rose like music on the ear.
Light from the full fount of glory
On his robes of whiteness glistened,
And the bright-winged seraphs near him
Bowed their radiant heads and listened.

"Lord, from Thy throne of glory here,
My heart turns fondly to another ;
O Lord our God, the Comforter,
Comfort, comfort, *my sweet mother !*
Many sorrows hast Thou sent her,
Meekly has she drained the cup ;
And the jewels Thou hast lent her
Unrepining yielded up.
Comfort, comfort, *my sweet mother !*

"Earth is growing lonely round her ;
Friend and lover hast Thou taken ;
Let her not, though woes surround her,
Feel herself by Thee forsaken.

Let her think, when faint and weary,
  We are waiting for her *here :*
Let each loss that makes earth dreary
  Make the hope of heaven more dear.
        Comfort, comfort, *my sweet mother !*

" Thou who once in nature human,
  Dwelt on earth a little child,
Pillowed on the breast of woman,
  Blessed Mary ! undefiled :
Thou who, from the cross of suffering,
  Marked Thy mother's tearful face,
And bequeathed her to Thy loved one,
  Bidding him to fill Thy place :
        Comfort, comfort, *my sweet mother !*

" Thou who once, from heaven descending,
  Tears and woes and conflicts won :
Thou who, Nature's laws suspending,
  Gavest the widow back her son :
Thou who at the grave of Lazarus
  Wept with those who wept their dead :
Thou who once in mortal anguish
  Bowed Thine own anointed head :
        Comfort, comfort, *my sweet mother !* "

The dove-like murmurs died away
  Upon the radiant air,
But still the little suppliant knelt,
  With hands still claspéd in prayer ;

Still were those mildly-pleading eyes
　　Turned to the sapphire throne,
Till golden harp and angel voice
　　Rang forth in mingled tone.
And as the swelling numbers flowed,
　　By angel voices given,
Rich, sweet, and clear, the anthem rolled
　　Through all the courts of heaven.
" He is the widow's God," it said,
　　"Who spared not His own Son !"
The infant cherub bowed his head—
　　" Thy will, *O Lord! be done.*"

＊＊

"It is I; be not afraid."

MATT. xiv. 37.

TOSSED with rough winds and faint with fear,
Above the tempest, soft and clear, .
What still small accents greet mine ear ?　.
　　　"'Tis I ; be not afraid."

"'Tis I, who led thy steps aright ;
'Tis I, who gave thy blind eyes sight ;
'Tis I, thy Lord, thy Life, thy Light.
　　　'Tis I ; be not afraid.

" These raging winds, this surging sea,
Bear not a breath of wrath to thee ;
That storm has all been spent on me.
　　　'Tis I ; be not afraid.

"This bitter cup fear not to drink;
I know it well—oh! do not shrink;
I tasted it o'er Kedron's brink.
　　　'Tis I; be not afraid.

"Mine eyes are watching by thy bed,
Mine arms are underneath thy head,
My blessing is around thee shed.
　　　'Tis I; be not afraid.

"When on the other side thy feet
Shall rest 'mid thousand welcomes sweet,
One well-known voice thy heart shall greet,
　　　'Tis I; be not afraid."

From out the dazzling majesty,
Gently He'll lay His hand on thee,
Whispering: "Beloved, lov'st thou me?
'Twas not in vain I died for thee.
　　　'Tis I; be not afraid."

Nature and Faith.

2 COR. iv. 17, 18.

WE wept—'twas *Nature* wept; but Faith
Can pierce beyond the gloom of death,
And in yon world, so fair and bright,
Behold thee in refulgent light!
We miss thee here, yet *Faith* would rather
Know thou art with thy Heavenly Father.

Nature sees the body dead—
Faith beholds the spirit fled ;
Nature stops at Jordan's tide—
Faith beholds the other side ;
That but hears farewell and sighs—
This thy welcome in the skies ;
Nature mourns a *cruel* blow—
Faith assures it is not so ;
Nature never sees thee more—
Faith but sees thee gone before ;
Nature tells a dismal story—
Faith has visions full of glory ;
Nature views the change with sadness—
Faith contemplates it with gladness ;
Nature murmurs—*Faith* gives meekness,
" Strength is perfected in weakness ; "
Nature writhes, and hates the rod—
Faith looks up and blesses God ;
Sense looks downwards—*Faith* above ;
That sees harshness—*this* sees love.
Oh ! let *Faith* victorious be—
Let it reign triumphantly !

But thou art gone ! not lost, but flown !
Shall I then ask thee back, my own ?
Back—and leave thy spirit's brightness ?
Back—and leave thy robes of whiteness ?
Back—and leave thine angel mould ?
Back—and leave those streets of gold ?

Back—and leave the Lamb who feeds thee?
Back—from founts to which He leads thee?
Back—and leave thy Heavenly Father;
Back—to earth and sin?—Nay; rather
Would I live in solitude!
I *would* not ask thee if I *could;*
But patient wait the high decree,
That calls my spirit home to thee!

———•———

My Lambs.

I LOVED them so,
That when the Elder Shepherd of the fold
Came, covered with the storm, and pale and cold,
And begged for one of my sweet lambs to hold,
       I bade Him go.

       He claimed the pet—
A little fondling thing, that to my breast
Clung always, either in quiet or unrest;
I thought of all my lambs I loved him best,
       And yet—and yet—

       I laid him down
In those white, shrouded arms, with bitter tears;
For some voice told me that, in after years,
He should know naught of passion, grief, or fears,
       As I had known.

·And yet again
That Elder Shepherd came.   My heart grew
    faint.
He claimed another lamb, with sadder plaint—
Another! She who, gentle as a saint,
    Ne'er gave me pain.

    Aghast I turned away!
There sat she, lovely as an angel's dream,
Her golden locks with sunlight all a-gleam,
Her holy eyes with heaven in their beam.
    I knelt to pray.

    " Is it Thy will,
My Father! say, must this pet lamb be given ?
Oh! Thou hast many such, dear Lord, in heaven."
And a soft voice said: "Nobly hast thou striven;
    But—peace, be still ! "

    Oh ! how I wept,
And clasped her to my bosom, with a wild
And yearning love—my lamb, my pleasant child!
Her, too, I gave.   The little angel smiled,
    And slept.

    "Go ! go !" I cried ;
For once again that Shepherd laid His hand
Upon the noblest of our household band ;
Like a pale spectre, there He took His stand,
    Close to his side.

And yet how wondrous sweet
The look with which He heard my passionate cry,
"Touch not my lamb ; for him, oh, let me die!"
"A little while," He said, with smile and sigh,
      "Again to meet."

Hopeless I fell ;
And when I rose, the light had burned so low,
So faint, I could not see my darling go :
He had not bidden me farewell, but oh !
      I felt farewell,

More deeply far
Than if my arms had compassed that slight
    frame ;
Though could I but have heard him call my
    name—
"Dear mother !"—but in heaven 'twill be the
    same:
      There burns my star !

He will not take
Another lamb, I thought, for only one
Of the dear fold is spared, to be my sun,
My guide, my mourner when this life is done :
      My heart would break.

Oh ! with what thrill
I heard Him enter ; but I did not know
(For it was dark) that He had robbed me so.
The idol of my soul, he could not go—
      O heart ! be still !

Çame morning.   Can I tell
How this poor frame its sorrowful tenant kept?
For waking tears were mine; I, sleeping, wept,
And days, months, years, that weary vigil kept.
    Alas! "Farewell!"

How often it is said!
I sit and think, and wonder too, sometime,
How it will seem, when, in that happier clime,
It never will ring out like funeral chime
    Over the dead.

No tears! no tears!
Will there a day come that I shall not weep?
For I bedew my pillow in my sleep.
Yes, yes; thank God! no grief that clime shall
    keep,
    No weary years.

Ay! it is well:
Well with my lambs, and with their earthly
    guide
There, pleasant rivers wander they beside,
Or strike sweet harps upon its silver tide—
    Ay! it is well.

Through the dreary day,
They often come from glorious light to me;
I cannot feel their touch, their faces see,
Yet my soul whispers they do come to me
    Heaven is not far away.

The Call.

THE night was dark; behold, the shade was
    deeper,
  In the old garden of Gethsemane,
When that calm voice awoke the weary sleeper :
  "Couldst thou not watch one hour alone
    with me?"

O thou ! so weary of thy self-denials,
  And so impatient of thy little cross,
Is it so hard to bear thy daily trials,
  To count all earthly things a gainful loss ?

What if thou *always* suffer tribulation,
  And if thy Christian warfare never cease ?
The gaining of the quiet habitation
  Shall gather thee to everlasting peace.

But here we all must suffer, walking lonely
  The path that Jesus once Himself hath gone :
Watch thou in patience, through the dark hour
    only—
  This one dark hour—before the eternal dawn.

The captive's oar may pause upon the galley,
  The soldier sleep beneath his plumèd crest,
And Peace may fold her wings o'er hill and
    valley ;
  But thou, O Christian ! must not take thy rest.

Thou must walk on, however man upbraid
 thee,
 With Him who trod the wine-press all alone;
Thou wilt not find one human hand to aid
 thee,
 One human soul to comprehend thine own.

Heed not the images for ever thronging
 From out the foregone life thou liv'st no
  more;
Faint-hearted mariner! still art thou longing
 For the dim line of the receding shore.

Wilt thou find rest of soul in thy returning
 To that old path thou hast so vainly trod?
Hast thou forgotten all thy weary yearning
 To walk among the children of thy God:

Faithful and steadfast in their consecration,
 Living by that high faith to thee so dim,
Declaring before God their dedication,
 So far from thee because so near to Him?

Canst thou forget thy Christian superscription,
 " Behold, we count them happy which
  endure?"
What treasure wouldst thou, in the land
 Egyptian,
 Repass the stormy water to secure?

And wilt thou yield thy sure and glorious
    promise
For the poor, fleeting joys earth can afford?
No hand can take away the treasure from us,
    That rests within the keeping of the Lord.

Poor wandering soul! I know that thou art
    seeking
Some easier way, as all have sought before,
To silence the reproachful inward speaking—
    Some landward path unto an island shore.

The cross is heavy in thy human measure,
    The way too narrow for thine inward pride;
Thou canst not lay thine intellectual treasure
    At the low footstool of the Crucified.

Oh! that my faithless soul, one great hour only
    Would comprehend the Christian's perfect
    life!
Despised with Jesus, sorrowful and lonely,
    Yet calmly looking upward in its strife!

For poverty and self-renunciation,
    The Father yielded back a thousand-fold;
In the calm stillness of regeneration,
    Cometh a joy we never knew of old.

In meek obedience to the Heavenly Teacher
    Thy weary soul can find its only peace;
Seeking no aid from any human creature—
    Looking to God alone for His release.

And He will come, in His own time and power,
   To set His earnest-hearted children free:
Watch only through this dark and painful hour,
   And the bright morning yet will break for thee.

—⊷—

God's Anvil.

PAIN'S furnace-heat within me quivers,
   God's breath upon the fire doth blow,
And all my heart in anguish shivers,
   And trembles at the fiery glow;
And yet I whisper, "As God will!"
And in His hottest fire hold still.

He comes, and lays my heart, all heated,
   On the bare anvil, minded so
Into His own fair shape to beat it,
   With His great hammer, blow on blow;
And yet I whisper, "As God will!"
And at His heaviest blows hold still.

He takes my softened heart, and beats it;
   The sparks fly off at every blow;
He turns it o'er and o'er, and heats it,
   And lets it cool, and makes it glow:
And yet I whisper, "As God will!"
And in His mighty hand hold still.

F

Why should I murmur? for the sorrow
    Thus only longer-lived would be;
Its end may come, and will to-morrow,
    When God has done His work in me:
So I say, trusting, "As God will!"
And, trusting to the end, hold still.

He kindles, for my profit purely,
    Afflictions glowing, fiery brand;
And all His heaviest blows are surely
    Inflicted by a master-hand:
So I say, praying, "As God will!"
And hope in Him, and suffer still.

———‡———

The Cross and Crown.

MUST Jesus bear the cross alone,
    And all the world go free?
No; there's a cross for every one,
    And there's a cross for me.

How happy are the saints above,
    Who once went sorrowing here;
But now they taste unmingled love
    And joy without a tear.

The consecrated cross I'll bear,
    Till death shall set me free;
And then go home, my crown to wear,
    For there's a crown for me.

Upon the crystal pavement, down
  At Jesus' piercèd feet,
Joyful I'll cast my golden crown,
  And His dear name repeat;

And palms shall wave, and harps shall ring,
  Beneath Heaven's arches high:
"The Lord that lives," the ransomed sing,
  "That lives no more to die."

——♦——

Even Me.

LORD! I hear of showers of blessing
  Thou art scattering full and free—
Showers the thirsty soul refreshing;
  Let some droppings fall on me,
                    Even me.

Pass me not, O gracious Father!
  Lost and sinful though I be;
Thou might'st curse me, but the rather
  Let Thy mercy light on me,
                    Even me.

Pass me not, O tender Saviour!
  Let me love and cling to Thee:
Fain I'm longing for Thy favour;
  When Thou callest, call for me,
                    Even me.

Pass me not, O mighty Spirit!
    Thou canst make the blind to see;
Testify of Jesus' merit,
    Speak the word of peace to me,
                Even me.

Have I long in sin been sleeping,
    Long been slighting, grieving Thee?
Has the world my heart been keeping?
    Oh! forgive and rescue me,
                Even me.

Love of God! so pure and changeless;
    Love of Christ! so rich and free;
Grace of God! so strong and boundless,
    Magnify it all in me,
                Even me.

Pass me not, Almighty Spirit!
    Draw this lifeless heart to Thee;
Impute to me the Saviour's merits;
    Blessing others, oh! bless me,
                Even me.

O my Saviour, Crucified!

O MY Saviour, crucified!
Near Thy cross may I abide;
There to gaze, with steadfast eye,
On Thy dying agony.

Jesus, bruised and put to shame,
Tells me all the Father's name;
God is love, I surely know,
By my Saviour's depths of woe!

In His sinless soul's distress
I behold my guiltiness:
Oh! how vile my low estate,
Since my ransom was so great.

Dwelling on Mount Calvary,
Contrite shall my spirit be;
Rest and holiness shall find,
Fashioned like my Saviour's mind.

———⊷———

The Peace of God.

WE ask for peace, O Lord!
　Thy children ask Thy peace:
Not what the world calls rest,
　That toil and care should cease:
That through bright sunny hours
　Calm life should fleet away,
And tranquil night should fade
　　In smiling day.
It is not for such peace that we would
　pray.

We ask for peace, O Lord !
　Yet not to stand secure,
Girt round with iron pride,
　Contented to endure ;
Crushing the gentle strings
　That human hearts should know ;
Untouched by others' joys
　　　Or others' woe.
Thou, O dear Lord ! wilt never teach us so.

We ask Thy peace, O Lord !
　Through storm and fear and strife,
To light and guide us on
　Through a long, struggling life ;
While no success or gain
　Shall cheer the desperate fight,
Or nerve what the world calls
　　　Our wasted might ;
Yet pressing through the darkness to the light.

It is Thine own, O Lord !
　Who toil while others sleep ;
Who sow, with living care,
　What other hands shall reap :
They lean on Thee, entranced,
　In calm and perfect rest.
Give us that peace, O Lord !
　　　Divine and blest,
Thou keepest for those hearts that love
　Thee best.

Peace.

LIFE'S mystery—deep, restless as the ocean—
    Hath surged and wailed for ages to and fro ;
Earth's generations watch its ceaseless motion,
    As in and out its hollow moanings flow.
Shivering and yearning by that unknown sea,
Let my soul calm itself, O God ! in Thee.

Life's sorrows, with inexorable power,
    Sweep desolation o'er this mortal plain ;
And human loves and hopes fly as the chaff
    Borne by the whirlwind from the ripened
        grain.
Oh ! when before that blast my hopes all flee,
Let my soul calm itself, O Christ ! in Thee.

Between the mysteries of death and life
    Thou standest, loving guiding, not explaining ;
We ask, and Thou art silent ; yet we gaze,
    And our charmed hearts forget their drear
        complaining,
No crushing fate, no stony destiny ;
Thou " Lamb that hath been slain ! " we rest in
        Thee.

The many waves of thought, the mighty tides,
    The ground-swell that rolls up from other
        lands.

From far-off worlds, from dim, eternal shores,
　　Whose echo dashes o'er life's wave-worn
　　　　strands ;
This vague, dark tumult of the inner sea
Grows calm, grows bright, O risen Lord ! in
　　Thee.

Thy piercèd hand guides the mysterious wheels,
　　Thy thorn-crowned brow now wears the
　　　　crown of power ;
And when the dark enigma presseth sore,
　　Thy patient voice saith : "Watch with me
　　　　one hour."
As sinks the moaning river in the sea.
In silent peace, so sinks my soul in Thee.

—▸◂—

Prayer for Strength.

FATHER ! before Thy footstool kneeling,
　　Once more my heart goes up to Thee ;
For aid, for strength, to Thee appealing,
　　Thou who alone canst succour me.

Hear me ! for heart and flesh are failing—
　　My spirit yielding in the strife ;
And anguish, wild as unavailing,
　　Sweeps in a flood across my life.

Help me to stem the tide of sorrow;
   Help me to bear Thy chastening rod;
Give me endurance; let me borrow
   Strength from Thy promise, O my God!

Not mine the grief which words may lighten,
   Not mine the tears of common woe:
The pang with which my heartstrings tighten
   Only the All-seeing One may know.

And I am weak; my feeble spirit
   Shrinks from life's task in wild dismay;
Yet not that Thou that task wouldst spare it,
   My Father, do I dare to pray.

Into my soul Thy might infusing,
   Strengthening my spirit by Thine' own,
Help me—all other aid refusing— ·
   To cling to Thee, and Thee alone.

And oh! in my exceeding weakness,
   Make Thy strength perfect: Thou art strong!
Aid me to do Thy will with meekness,
   Thou, to whom all my powers belong.

Saviour! our human form once wearing,
   Help, by the memory of that day,
When, painfully Thy dark cross bearing,
   E'en for a time Thy strength gave way.

Beneath a lighter burden sinking,
   Jesus, I cast myself on Thee;
Forgive, forgive this useless shrinking
   From trials that I know must be.

Oh! let me feel that Thou art near me,
   Close to Thy side I shall not fear.
Hear me, O Strength of Israel! hear me!
   Sustain and aid! in mercy, hear!

—⋅—

Onward.

TRAVELLER! faint not on the road,
   Droop not in the parching sun;
Onward, onward with thy load,
   Till the night be won.
Swerve not, though thy bleeding feet
   Fain the narrow path would leave;
From the burden and the heat
   Thou shalt rest at eve.

'Midst a world that round thee fades
   Brightening stars and twilight life;
When a sacred calm pervades
   All that now is strife;
Rich the joy to be revealed
   In that hour from labour free,
Bright the splendours that shall yield
   Happiness to thee.

Master of a holy charm,
  Yet be patient on thy way;
Use the spell, and check the harm
  That would lead astray.
From the petty cares that teem,
  Turn thee, with prophetic eye,
To the glory of that dream
  Which shall never die.

By the mystery of thy trust;
  By the grandeur of that hour
When mortality and dust
  Clothed eternal power;
By the purple robe of shame,
  The mockery, and the insulting rod;
By the anguish that o'ercame
  The incarnate God:

Faint not! fail not! be thou strong,
  Cast away distrust and fear;
Though the weary day seems long,
  Yet the night is near.
Friends and kindred wait beyond—
  They who passed the trial pure:
Traveller, by that holy bond,
  Shrink not to endure!

Grief was sent thee for thy Good.

SOME there are who seem exempted
     From the doom incurred by all ;
Are they not more sorely tempted ?
     Are they not the first to fall ?
As a mother's firm denial
     Checks her infant's wayward mood,
Wisdom lurks in every trial—
     Grief was sent thee for thy good.

In the scenes of former pleasure,
     Present anguish hast thou felt ;
O'er thy fond heart's dearest treasure
     As a mourner hast thou knelt.
In thy hour of deep affliction,
     Let no impious thoughts intrude :
Meekly bow, with this conviction—
     Grief was sent thee for thy good.

Scenes "on Jordan's Strand."

THERE came a little child, with sunny hair,
     All fearless to the brink of Death's dark river,
And with a sweet confiding in the care
     Of Him who is of life the Joy and Giver ;
And, as upon the waves she left our sight,
We heard her say : " My Saviour makes them
          bright."

Next came a youth, with bearing most serene,
　Nor turned a single backward look of
　　sadness ;
But, as he left each gay and flowery scene,
　Smiling declared : " My soul is thrilled with
　　gladness !
What earth deems bright, for ever I resign,
　Joyful but this to know, that Christ is mine."

An aged mourner, trembling, tottered by,
　And paused a moment by the swelling river,
Then glided on beneath the shadowy sky,
　Singing : " Christ Jesus is my strength for
　　ever,
Upon His arm my feeble soul I lean ;
My glance meets His, without a cloud between."

And scarce her last triumphant note had died,
　Ere hastened on a man of wealth and learning,
Who cast at once his bright renown aside,
　These only words unto his friends returning :
" Christ for my wisdom thankfully I own,
And as ' a little child ' I seek His throne."

Then saw I this : that whether guileless child,
　Or youth, or age, or genius, won salvation,
Each self-renouncing came ; on each God
　　smiled ;
　Each found the love of Christ rich compen-
　　sation

For loss of friends, earth's pleasures, and
    renown ;
Each entered Heaven, and " by His side sat
    down."

———

There is Light beyond.

BEYOND the stars that shine in golden glory,
    Beyond the calm sweet moon,
Up the bright ladder saints have trod before
    thee,
    Soul ! thou shalt venture soon.
Secure with Him who sees thy heart-sick
    yearning,
    Safe in His arms of love,
Thou shalt exchange the midnight for the
    morning
    And thy fair home above.

Oh ! it is sweet to watch the world's night
    wearing,
    The Sabbath morn come on ;
And sweet it were the vineyard labour sharing—
    Sweeter the labour done.
All finished ! all the conflict and the sorrow ;
    Earth's dream of anguish o'er ;
Deathless there dawns for thee a nightless
    morrow
    On Eden's blissful shore.

Patience! then, patience!—soon the pang of
    dying
      Shall all forgotten be,
And thou, through rolling spheres rejoicing,
    flying
      Beyond the waveless sea,
Shalt know hereafter where thy Lord doth lead
    thee,
      His darkest dealings trace;
And by those fountains where His love will
    feed thee,
      Behold Him face to face.

Then bow thine head, and God shall give thee
    meekness,
      Bravely to do His will;
So shall arise His glory in thy weakness—
      O struggling soul! be still.
Dark clouds are His pavilion shining o'er thee,
      Thine heart must recognise
The veiled Shechinah moving on before thee,
      Too bright to meet thine eyes.

Behold the wheel that straightly moves, and
    fleetly
      Performs the Sovereign Word!
Thou know'st His suffering love! then suffering
    meekly,
      Follow thy loving Lord!

Watch on the tower, and listen by the gateway,
    Nor weep to wait alone ;
Take thou thy spices, and some angel straight-
        way
    Shall roll away the stone.

Then shalt thou tell thy living Lord hath risen,
    And risen but to save—
Tell of the might that breaks the captive's prison,
    And life beyond the grave—
Tell how He met thee, all His radiance
    shrouded ;
    How in thy sorrow came
His pitying voice, breathing, when faith was
    clouded,
    Thine own familiar name.

So at the grave's dark portal thou may'st linger,
    And hymn some happy strain :
The passing world may mock the feeble singer—
    Heed not, but sing again.
Thus wait, thus watch, till He the last link
    sever,
    And changeless rest be won ;
Then in His glory thou shalt bask for ever.
    Fear not the clouds—PRESS ON !

"Thy Will be Done."

FOUR little words, no more—
　Easy to say;
But thoughts that went before,
　Can words convey?

The struggle, only known
　To one proud soul,
And Him whose eye alone
　Has marked the whole,

Before that stubborn will
　At length was broke,
And a low "Peace, be still!"
　One soft Voice spoke;

The pang, when that sad heart
　Its dreams resigned,
And strength was found to part
　Those bonds long twined;

To yield that treasure up,
　So fondly clasped,
To drain that bitter cup,
　So sadly grasped!

But all is calm at last,
　"Thy will be done!"
Enough—the storm is past,
　The field is won.

G

Now for the peaceful breast,
  The quiet sleep ;
For soul and spirit rest,
  Tranquil and deep—

Rest, whose full bliss and power
  They only know
Who knew the bitter hour
  Of restless woe.

The rebel will subdued—
  The fond heart free—
" Thy will be done ! "—*all* good
  That comes from Thee.

All weary thought and care,
  Lord, we resign ;
Ours is to do, to bear—
  To choose is Thine.

Four little words, no more—
  Easy to say ;
But what was felt before,
  Can words convey ?

They shall be Mine!

".THEY shall be mine ! " Oh ! lay them down
    to slumber,
  Calm in the strong assurance that He gives :
He calls them by their names, He knows their
    number,
  And they shall live as surely as He lives.

" They shall be mine ! " upraised from earthly
    pillows,
  Gathered from desert sand, from mountains
    cold—
Called from the graves beneath old ocean's
    billows,
  Called from each distant land, each scattered
    fold.

Well might the soul, that wondrous spark of
    being,
  Lit by His breath who claims it for His own,
Shine in the circle which His love foreseeing
  Destined to glitter brightest by His throne.

But shall the dust from earthly dust first taken,
  And now long mingled with its native earth,
To life, to beauty, once again awaken,
  Thrill with the rapture of a second birth ?

"They shall be mine!"—they, as on earth we
    knew them—
   The lips we kissed, the hands we loved to
     press ;
Only a fuller life be circling through them—
   Unfading youth, unchanging holiness.

"They shall be mine!" Children of sin and
    sorrow,
   Giv'st Thou, O Lord! heaven's almost verge
     to them?
No; from each rifled grave Thy crown shall
    borrow
   An added light—a prized and costly gem.

"They shall be mine!" Thought fails and
    feeling falters,
   Striving to sound and fathom Love Divine :
All that we know—no time Thy promise alters ;
   All that we trust—our loved ones shall be
    Thine.

—— ⊶ ——

Leave me not Now.

LEAVE me not now, while still the shade is
    creeping
   O'er the sad heart that longs to rest in Thee ;
Hear my complaint, and while my soul is
    weeping,
   Breathe Thou the holy dew of sympathy.

Leave me not now, Thou Saviour of compassion,
  While yet the busy tempter lurketh near;
Lord, by Thine anguish and Thy wondrous
    passion,
  Do I entreat Thee now to linger here.

Jesus! Thou soul of love, Thou heart of feeling,
  Let me repose the weary night away
Safe on Thy bosom, all my woes revealing,
  Secure from danger, till the dawn of day.

Then leave me not, O Comforter and Father.
  Parent of love! I live but in Thy sight.
Good Shepherd! to Thy fold the wand'rer
    gather,
  There to adore Thee, morning, noon, and
    night.

Faith's Repose.

FATHER! beneath Thy sheltering wing,
  In sweet security we rest,
And fear no evil earth can bring,
  In life, in death, supremely. blest.

For life is good, whose tidal flow
  The motions of Thy will obeys;
And death is good, that makes us know
  The Love Divine that all things sways.

And good it is to bear the cross,
　　And so Thy perfect peace to win ;
And naught is ill, nor brings us loss,
　　Nor works us harm, save only sin.

Redeemed from this, we ask no more,
　　But trust the love that saves to guide :
The grace that yields so rich a store
　　Will grant us all we need beside.

—▸◂—

The Delectable Mountains.

I SEE them far away,
　　In their calm beauty, on the evening skies ;
Across the golden west their summits rise,
　　Bright with the radiance of departing day.
And often, ere the sunset light was gone,
Gazing and longing, I have hastened on,
As with new strength, all weariness and pain
Forgotten in the hope those blissful heights to
　　　gain.

　　Heaven lies not far beyond !
But these are hills of earth ; our changeful air
Circles around them, and the dwellers there
　　Still own mortality's mysterious bond,
The ceaseless contact, the continued strife,
Of sin and grace, which can but close with life,

Is not yet ended, and the Jordan's roar
Still sounds between their path and the Celestial
    shore.   .

    But there, the pilgrims say,
On these calm heights, the tumult and the noise
Of all our busy cares and restless joys
    Has almost in the distance died away ;
All the past journey "a right way" appears,
Thoughts of the future wake no faithless fears,
And through the clouds, to their rejoicing eyes,
The city's golden streets and pearly gates
    arise.

    Courage, poor fainting heart !
These happy ones in the far distance seen
Were sinful wanderers once, as thou hast been,
    Weary and sorrowful, as now thou art.
Linger no longer on the lonely plain ;
Press boldly onward, and thou too shalt gain
Their vantage-ground ; and then, with vigour
    new,
All thy remaining race and pilgrimage pursue.

    Ah ! far too faint, too poor
Are all our views and aims.   We only stand
Within the borders of the promised land ;
    Its precious things we seek not to secure :
And thus our hands hang down, and oft unstrung
Our harps are left the willow-trees among.

Lord ! lead us forward, upward, till we know
How much of heavenly bliss may be enjoyed
   below.

" And then, said they, we will, if the day be clear, show you
the Delectable Mountains. . . . . So he looked, and behold, at
a great distance he saw a most pleasant mountainous country,
. . . . very delectable to behold, ... and it is as common,
said they, as this hill is, to and for all the pilgrims. And when
thou comest there, from thence thou mayest see to the gate of
the Celestial City."—*Bunyan.*

The Anchor within the Veil.

AMID the shadows and the fears
That overcloud this home of tears,
Amid my poverty and sin,
The tempest and the war within,
     I cast my soul on Thee,
     Mighty to save e'en me,
     Jesus, Thou Son of God !

Drifting across a sunless sea,
Cold, heavy mist encurtaining me ;
Toiling along life's broken road,
With snares around, and foes abroad,
     I cast my soul on Thee,
     Mighty to save e'en me,
     Jesus, Thou Son of God !

Mine is a day of fear and strife,
A needy soul, a needy life,
A needy world, a needy age ;
Yet, in my perilous pilgrimage,
    I cast my soul on Thee,
    Mighty to save e'en me,
    Jesus, Thou Son of God !

To Thee I come—ah ! only Thou
Canst wipe the sweat from off this brow ;
Thou, only Thou, canst make me whole,
And soothe the fever of my soul ;
    I cast my soul on Thee,
    Mighty to save e'en me,
    Jesus, Thou Son of God !

On Thee I rest—Thy love and grace
Are my sole rock and resting-place ;
In Thee my thirst and hunger sore,
Lord, let me quench for evermore.
    I cast my soul on Thee,
    Mighty to save e'en me,
    Jesus, Thou Son of God !

'Tis earth, not heaven ; 'tis night, not noon ;
The sorrowless is coming soon :
But, till the morn of love appears,
Which ends the travail and the tears,
    I cast my soul on Thee,
    Mighty to save e'en me,
    Jesus, Thou Son of God !

God's Ways.

How few who from their youthful day
  Look on to what their life may be,
Painting the visions of the way
  In colours soft, and bright, and free—
How few who to such paths have brought
The hopes and dreams of early thought !
For God, through ways they have not known,
  Will lead His own.

The eager hearts, the souls of fire,
  Who pant to toil for God and man,
And view with eyes of keen desire
  The upland way of toil and pain ;
Almost with scorn they think of rest,
Of holy calm, of tranquil breast ;
But God, through ways they have not known,
  Will lead His own.

A lowlier task on them is laid,
  With love to make the labour light ;
And then their beauty they must shed
  On quiet homes and lost to sight.
Changed are their visions high and fair,
Yet calm and still they labour there ;
For God, through ways they have not known,
  Will lead His own.

The gentle heart that thinks with pain
   It scarce can lowliest tasks fulfil,
And, if it dared its life to scan,
   Would ask but pathway low and still,
Often such lowly heart is brought
To act with power beyond its thought ;
For God, through ways they have not known,
     Will lead His own.

And they the bright, who long to prove
   In joyous path, in cloudless lot,
How fresh from earth their grateful love
   Can spring without a stain or spot ;
Often such youthful heart is given
The path of grief to walk to heaven ;
For God, through ways they have not known,
     Will lead His own.

What matter what the path shall be ?
   The end is clear and bright to view :
He knows that we a strength shall see
   Whate'er the day shall bring to do :
We see the end, the house of God,
But not the path to that abode ;
For God, through ways they have not known,
     Will lead His own.

Distractions in Prayer.

I CANNOT pray; yet, Lord, Thou know'st
   The pain it is to me,
To have my vainly struggling thoughts
   Thus torn away from Thee.

Prayer was not meant for luxury
   Of selfish pastime sweet;
It is the prostrate creature's place
   At his Creator's feet.

Had I, dear Lord, no pleasure found
   But in the thoughts of Thee,
Prayer would have come unsought, and been
   A truer liberty.

Yet Thou art oft most present, Lord,
   In weak distracted prayer;
A sinner out of heart with self
   Most often finds Thee there.

And prayer that humbles sets the soul
   From all illusions free,
And teaches it how utterly,
   Dear Lord, it hangs on Thee.

The soul that on self-sacrifice
   Is dutifully bent,
Will bless the chastening hand that makes
   Its prayer its punishment.

Ah, Jesus ! why should I complain ?
  And why fear aught but sin ?
Distractions are but outward things ;
  Thy peace dwells far within !

These surface troubles come and go
  Like rufflings of the sea ;
The deeper depth is out of reach
  To all, my God, but Thee !

My Guest.

I HAVE a wonderful Guest,
  Who speeds my feet, who moves my hands,
Who strengthens, comforts, guides, commands,
  Whose presence gives me rest.

He dwells within my soul ;
He swept away the filth and gloom,
He garnished fair the empty room,
  And now pervades the whole.

For aye, by day and night,
He keeps the portal—suffers naught
Defile the temple He has bought,
  And filled with joy and light.

Once 'twas a cavern dim;
The home of evil thoughts, desires,
Enkindled by infernal fires,
    Without one thought of Him.

Regenerated by His grace,
Still 'tis a meagre inn, at best,
Wherein the King's to make His rest,
    And show His glorious face.

Yet, Saviour, ne'er depart
From this poor earthly cottage home,
Until the Father bid me come,
    Whisp'ring within my heart:

" I shake these cottage walls;
Fear not ! at my command they bow !
My heavenly mansions open now,
    As this poor dwelling falls."

Then my dear wondrous Guest
Shall bear me on His own right hand
Unto that fair and Promised Land,
    Where I in Him shall rest.

Coming.

"At even, or at midnight, or at the cock-crowing, or in the
morning."

" IT may be in the evening,
    When the work of the day is done
And you have time to sit in the twilight
    And watch the sinking sun,
While the long, bright day dies slowly
    Over the sea,
And the hour grows quiet and holy
    With thoughts of me ;
While you hear the village children
    Passing along the street,
Among those thronging footsteps
    May come the sound of *my* feet.
Therefore I tell you : Watch
    By the light of the evening-star,
When the room is growing dusky
    As the clouds afar ;
Let the door be on the latch
    In your home,
For it may be through the gloaming
    I will come.

"It may be when the midnight
    Is heavy upon the land,

And the black waves lying dumbly
    Along the sand ;
When the moonless night draws close,
And the lights are out in the house ;
When the fires burn low and red,
And the watch is ticking loudly
    Beside the bed.
Though you sleep, tired out, on your couch,
Still your heart must wake and watch
    In the dark room ;
For it may be that at midnight
    I will come.

" It may be at the cockcrow,
  When the night is dying slowly
    In the sky,
And the sea looks calm and holy,
    Waiting for the dawn
    Of the golden sun
    Which draweth nigh ;
When the mists are on the valleys, shading
    The rivers chill,
And my morning-star is fading, fading
    Over the hill :
Behold I say unto you : Watch !
Let the door be on the latch
    In your home ;
In the chill before the dawning,
Between the night and morning,
    I may come.

" It may be in the morning,
        When the sun is bright and strong,
And the dew is glittering sharply
        Over the little lawn ;
When the waves are laughing loudly
        Along the shore,
And the little birds are singing sweetly
        About the door ;
With the long day's work before you,
        You rise up with the sun,
And the neighbours come in to talk a little
        Of all that must be done :
But remember that *I* may be the next
        To come in at the door,
To call you from all your busy work
        . For evermore.
As you work your heart must watch ;
For the door is on the latch
        In your room,
And it may be in the morning
        I will come."

So He passed down my cottage garden,
        By the path that leads to the sea,
Till He came to the turn of the little road
        Where the birch and laburnum tree
Lean over and arch the way ;
There I saw Him a moment stay,
        And turn once more to me,
        As I wept at the cottage door,

H

And lift up His hands in blessing—
    Then I saw His face no more.

And I stood still in the doorway,
    Leaning against the wall,
Not heeding the fair white roses,
    Though I crushed them and let them fall.
Only looking down the pathway,
    And looking toward the sea,
And wondering, and wondering
    When He would come back for me;
Till I was aware of an angel
    Who was going swiftly by,
With the gladness of one who goeth
    In the light of God Most High.

He passed the end of the cottage
    Toward the garden gate—
(I suppose he was come down
At the setting of the sun,
To comfort some one in the village
    Whose dwelling was desolate)—
And he paused before the door
    Beside my place,
And the likeness of a smile
    Was on his face:
"Weep not," he said, "for unto you is given
    To watch for the coming of His feet
Who is the glory of our blessed heaven;

The work and watching will be very sweet,
    Even in an earthly home ;
And in such an hour as you think not,
    He will come."

So I am watching quietly
    Every day.
Whenever the sun shines brightly,
    I rise and say :
"Surely it is the shining of His face !"
And look unto the gates of His high place
    Beyond the sea ;
For I know He is coming shortly
    To summon me.
And when a shadow falls across the window
    'Of my room,
Where I am working my appointed task,
I lift my head to watch the door, and ask
    If He is come ;
And the angel answers sweetly
    In my home :
"Only a few more shadows,
    And He will come."

A Quiet Mind.

I HAVE a treasure which I prize;
   Its like I cannot find:
There's nothing like it on the earth;
   'Tis this—a quiet mind.

But 'tis not that I'm stupefied,
   Or senseless, dull, or blind;
'Tis God's own peace within my heart,
   Which forms my quiet mind.

I found this treasure at the cross:
   And there, to every kind
Of weary, heavy-laden souls,
   Christ gives a quiet mind.

My Saviour's death and risen life
   To give it were designed;
His love, the never-failing spring
   Of this my quiet mind.

The love of God within my breast,
   My heart to Him doth bind;
This is the peace of heaven on earth—
   This is my quiet mind.

I've many a cross to take up now,
   And many left behind;
But present troubles move me not,
   Nor shake my quiet mind.

And what may be to-morrow's cross,
   I never seek to find ;
My Saviour says : " Leave that to me,
   And keep a quiet mind."

And well I know the Lord hath said,
   To make my heart resigned,
That mercy still shall follow those
   Who have this quiet mind.

I meet with pride of wit and wealth,
   And scorn, and looks unkind ;
It matters not—I envy none,
   While I've a quiet mind.

I'm waiting now to see my Lord,
   So patient and so kind ;
I want to thank Him face to face,
   For this my quiet mind.

—+—

All is Light.

WHAT though storm-clouds gather round me,
   Hovering darkly o'er my way ?
While I see the cross of Calvary
   Beaming with celestial ray,
     All is light, all is light !

What though mortal powers may falter?
    Earthly plans and prospects fail?
With a heaven-born hope which entereth
    E'en to that within the veil,
        All is light, all is light!

What though all my future pathway
    Be from mortal sight concealed?
With the love of Jesus glowing,
    As it lies to faith revealed,
        All is light, all is light!

E'en though death's deep vale before me
    Seem o'erspread with thickest gloom,
While I see a heavenly radiance
    Bursting from beyond the tomb,
        All is light, all is light!

—◦—

Longings.

WHEN shall I be at rest?   My trembling heart
    Grows weary of its burden, sickening still
    With hopes deferred. Oh! that it were Thy
        will
To loose my bonds, and take me where Thou
        art!

When shall I be at rest ?   My eyes grow dim
  With straining through the gloom ; I scarce
    can see
The waymarks that my Saviour left for me.
Would it were morn, and I were safe with
  Him !

When shall I be at rest?   Hand over hand
  I grasp, and climb an ever-steeper hill,
  A rougher path.   Oh! that it were Thy will
My tired feet might tread the Promised Land !

Oh ! that I were at rest !   A thousand fears
  Come thronging o'er me, lest I fall at last.
  Would I were safe, all toil and danger past.
And Thine own hands might wipe away my
    tears !

Oh ! that I were at rest, like some I love,
  Whose last fond looks drew half my life
    away,
  Seeming to plead that either they might stay
With me on earth, or I with them above.

But why these murmurs ?   Thou didst never
    shrink
  From any toil or weariness for me—
  Not even from that last deep agony :
Shall I beneath my little trials sink ?

No, Lord ; for when I am indeed at rest,
　　One taste of that deep bliss will quite efface
　　The sternest memories of my earthly race,
Save but to swell the sense of being blest.

Then lay on me whatever cross I need
　　To bring me there.　I know Thou canst not be
　　Unkind, unfaithful, or untrue to me !
Shall I not toil for Thee, when Thou for me
　　　　didst bleed ?

—⋈—

Bridges.

I HAVE a bridge within my heart,
　　Known as the Bridge of Sighs ;
It stretches from life's sunny part,
　　To where its darkness lies.

And when upon this bridge I stand,
　　To watch life's tide below,
Sad thoughts come from the shadowy land,
　　And darken all its flow.

Then, as it winds its way along
　　To sorrow's bitter sea,
. Oh ! mournful is the spirit-song
　　That upward floats to me.

A song which breathes of blessings dead,
  Of friends and friendships flown,
And pleasures gone—their distant tread,
  Now to an echo grown.

And hearing thus, beleaguering fears
  Soon shut the present out,
While joy but in the past appears,
  And in the future doubt.

Oh ! often then will deeper grow,
  The night that round me lies ;
I wish that life had run its flow ;
  Or never found its rise !

I have a bridge within my heart,
  Known as the Bridge of Faith ;
It spans, by a mysterious art,
  The streams of life and death.

And when upon this bridge I stand,
  To watch the tide below,
Sweet thoughts come from the sunny land,
  And brighten all its flow.

Then, as it winds its way along
  Down to a distant sea,
Oh ! pleasant is the spirit-song
  That upward floats to me.

A song of blessings never sere,
   Of love " beyond compare,"
Of pleasures flowed from troublings here,
   To rise serenely there.

And, hearing thus, a peace divine
   Soon shuts each sorrow out ;
And all is hopeful and benign,
   Where all was fear and doubt.

Oh ! often then will brighter grow,
   The light that round me lies,
I see from life's beclouded flow
   A crystal stream arise.

" Father, take my Hand."

THE way is dark, my Father ! Cloud on cloud
Is gathering thickly o'er my head, and loud
The thunders roar above me. See, I stand
Like one bewildered ! Father, take my hand,
     And through the gloom
     Lead safely home
     Thy child !

The day goes fast, my Father ! and the night
Is drawing darkly down. My faithless sight

Sees ghostly visions : fears, a spectral band,
Encompass me.   O Father ! take my hand,
   And from the night
   Lead up to light
    Thy child !

The way is long, my Father ! and my soul
Longs for the rest and quiet of the goal
While yet I journey through this weary land,
Keep me from wandering.   Father, take my
  hand ;
   Quickly and straight
   Lead to heaven's gate
    Thy child !

The path is rough, my Father ! Many a thorn
Has pierced me ; and my weary feet, all torn
And bleeding, mark the way. Yet Thy command
Bids me press forward.   Father, take my hand ;
   Then, safe and blest,
   Lead up to rest
    Thy child !

The throng is great, my Father ! Many a doubt
And fear and danger compass me about,
And foes oppress me sore.   I cannot stand
Or go alone.   O Father ! take my hand,
   And through the throng
   Lead safe along
    Thy child !

The cross is heavy, Father! I have borne
It long, and still do bear it. Let my worn
And fainting spirit rise to that blest land
Where crowns are given. Father, take my hand;
  And, reaching down,
  Lead to the crown
   Thy child!

—✴—

The Gracious Answer.

The way is dark, my child! but leads to light.
I would not always have thee walk by sight.
My dealings now thou canst not understand;
I meant it so; but I will take thy hand,
  And through the gloom
  Lead safely home
   My child!

The day goes fast, my child! But is the night
Darker to me than day? In me is light!
Keep close to me, and every spectral band
Of fears shall vanish. I will take thy hand,
  And through the night
  Lead up to light
   My child!

The way is long, my child! But it shall be
Not one step longer than is best for thee;

And thou shalt know, at last, when thou shalt
    stand
Safe at the goal, how I did take thy hand,
        And quick and straight
        Lead to heaven's gate
        My child!

The path is rough, my child! But oh! how
    sweet
Will be the rest, for weary pilgrims meet,
When thou shalt reach the borders of that land,
To which I lead thee, as I take thy hand,
        And safe and blest
        With me shalt rest
        My child!

The throng is great, my child! But at thy side
Thy Father walks : then be not terrified,
For I am with thee ; will thy foes command
To let thee freely pass ; will take thy hand
        And through the throng
        Lead safe along
        My child!

The cross is heavy, child! Yet there was One
Who bore a heavier for thee—my Son,
My well-beloved. For Him bear thine; and stand
With Him at last; and, from thy Father's hand,
        Thy cross laid down,
        Receive a crown,
        My child!

Oroomiah, Persia.   H. N. O.

Asleep on Guard.

"OH, shame!" we're sometimes fain to say
On Peter sleeping, while his dear Lord lay
Awake with anguish in the garden's shade,
Waiting His hour to be betrayed.

We say, or think, if we had gone
Thither—instead of Peter, James, and John—
And Christ had left us on the outpost dim,
As sentinels to watch with Him;

We would have sooner died than sleep
The little time we vigil had to keep;
Then wake to feel His torturing question's
     power,
"Could ye not watch with me one hour?"

One hour in sad Gethsemane!
And such an hour as that to Him must be!
All night our tireless eyes had pierced the shade,
Where He in grief's great passion prayed.

What do we now, to make our word
Seem no vain boast of love to Christ our Lord?
We cannot take the chidden sleeper's place,
And shun, by proof, his deep disgrace!

No more, the olive's shade beneath,
The human Christ foretastes the cup of death,

And leaves His servants in the outer gloom,
To watch till He again shall come!

Yet are there midnights dark and dread,
When Jesus still by traitors is betrayed;
Our bosom-sin's the lurking foe at hand,
And "Watch with me" is Christ's command.

One little hour of sleepless care,
And sin could wrest no victory from us there;
But, with the fame of our loved Lord to keep,
Like those we scorn, we fall asleep.

Oh! if our risen Lord must chide
Our souls for slumbering His death-cross beside,
What face have we to boast our feeble sense
Had shamed poor Peter's vigilance!

On Peter, James, and John, no more
The wrong reproach of hasty pride we pour;
But feel within the question's torturing power,
"Could *ye* not watch with me one hour?"

———

The Hour of Prayer.

My God, is any hour so sweet,
   From blush of morn to evening star,
As that which calls me to Thy feet—
   The hour of prayer!

Blest is that tranquil hour of morn,
　　And blest that hour of solemn eve,
When, on the wings of faith up-borne,
　　The world I leave !

For then a day-spring shines on me,
　　Brighter than morn's ethereal glow ;
And richer dews descend from Thee
　　Than earth can know.

Then is my strength by Thee renewed ;
　　Then do I feel my sins forgiven
Then dost Thou cheer my solitude
　　With joys of heaven.

No words can tell what sweet relief
　　There for my every want I find ;
What strength for warfare, balm for grief,
　　What peace of mind.

Hushed is each doubt, gone every fear ;
　　My spirit seems in heaven to stay ;
And e'en the penitential tear
　　Is wiped away.

Lord ! till I reach that blissful shore,
　　No privilege so dear shall be,
As thus my inmost soul to pour
　　In prayer to Thee.

Thy Will be Done.

WE see not, know not. All our way
Is night. With Thee alone is day.
From out the torrent's troubled drift,
Above the storm our prayers we lift—
  Thy will be done !

The flesh may fail, the heart may faint,
But who are we, to make complaint,
Or dare to plead, in times like these,
The weakness of our love of ease ?
  Thy will be done !

We take with solemn thankfulness
Our burden up, nor ask it less ;
And count it joy that even we
May suffer, serve, or wait for Thee,
  Whose will be done ! .

Though dim, as yet, in tint and line,
We trace Thy picture's wise design,
And thank Thee that our age supplies
Its dark relief of sacrifice—
  Thy will be done !

And if, in our unworthiness,
Thy sacrificial wine we press ;
If, from Thy ordeal's heated bars,
Our feet are seamed with crimson scars,
  Thy will be done !

I

If, for the age to come, this hour
Of trial hath vicarious power;
And, blest by Thee, our present pain
Be Liberty's eternal gain,
       Thy will be done !

Strike ! Thou the Master, we Thy keys,
The anthem of the destinies !
The minor of Thy loftier strain,
Our hearts shall breathe the old refrain—
       Thy will be done !

—⋈—

Hymn of Trust.

O LOVE DIVINE ! that stooped to share
   Our sharpest pang, our bitterest tear,
On Thee we cast each earth-born care;
   We smile at pain while Thou art near !

Though long the weary way we tread,
   And sorrows crown each lingering year,
No path we shun, no darkness dread,
   Our hearts still whispering, Thou art near!

When drooping pleasure turns to grief,
   And trembling faith is changed to fear,
The murmuring wind, the quivering leaf,
   Shall softly tell us, Thou art near !

On Thee we fling our burdening woe,
 O Love Divine! for ever dear;
Content to suffer, while we know,
 Living and dying Thou art near!

—*—

The Burial of Moses.

By Nebo's lonely mountain,
 On this side Jordan's wave,
In a vale in the land of Moab,
 There lies a lonely grave;
And no man dug that sepulchre,
 And no man saw it e'er,
For the "Sons of God" upturned the sod,
 And laid the dead man there.

That was the grandest funeral
 That ever passed on earth;
But no man heard the trampling,
 Or saw the train go forth.
Noiselessly as the daylight
 Comes when the night is done,
And the crimson streak on ocean's cheek
 Grows into the great sun—

Noiselessly as the spring-time
 Her crown of verdure weaves,
And all the trees on all the hills
 Open their thousand leaves;

So, without sound of music,
   Or voice of them that wept,
Silently down from the mountain's crown
   The great procession swept.

Perchance the bald old eagle,
   On gray Beth-peor's height,
Out of his rocky eyry
   Looked on the wondrous sight ;
Perchance the lion stalking
   Still shuns that hallowed spot :
For beast and bird have seen and heard
   That which man knoweth not.

But when the warrior dieth,
   His comrades in the war,
With arms reversed, and muffled drum,
   Follow the funeral car ;
They show the banners taken,
   They tell his battles won,
And after him lead his masterless steed,
   While peals the minute-gun.

Amid the noblest of the land
   Men lay the sage to rest,
And give the bard an honoured place,
   With costly marble drest—
In the great minster transept,
   Where lights like glories fall,

And the sweet choir sings, and the organ
    rings,
Along the emblazoned wall,

This was the bravest warrior
    That ever buckled sword ;
This, the most gifted poet
    That ever breathed a word ;
And never earth's philosopher
    Traced with his golden pen,
On the deathless page, truths half so sage
    As he wrote down for men.

And had he not high honour ?
    The hill-side for his pall,
To lie in state, while angels wait
    With stars for tapers tall,
And the dark rock-pines, like tossing plumes,
    Over his bier to wave,
And God's own hand, in that lonely land,
    To lay him in the grave !

In that deep grave without a name,
    Whence his uncoffined clay
Shall break again—most wondrous thought—
    Before the Judgment-day,
And stand, with glory wrapped around,
    On the hills he never trod,
And speak of the strife that won our life
    With the Incarnate Son of God.

Oh, lonely tomb in Moab's land !
    Oh, dark Beth-peor hill !
Speak to these curious hearts of ours,
    And teach them to be still.
God hath His mysteries of grace,
    Ways that we cannot tell ;
And hides them deep, like the secret sleep
    Of him He loved so well.

"Now."

" RISE ! for the day is passing,
    And you lie dreaming on ;
The others have buckled their armour,
    And forth to the fight are gone :
A place in the ranks awaits you ;
    Each man has some part to play ;
The Past and Future are looking
    In the face of the stern To-day."

The Need of Jesus.

I NEED Thee, precious Jesus !
    For I am full of sin ;
My soul is dark and guilty,
    My heart is dead within.

I need the cleansing fountain,
  Where I can always flee—
The blood of Christ most precious,
  The sinner's perfect plea.

I need Thee, precious Jesus!
  For I am very poor;
A stranger and a pilgrim,
  I have no earthly store.
I need the love of Jesus,
  To cheer me on my way,
To guide my doubting footsteps,
  To be my strength and stay.

I need Thee, precious Jesus!
  I need a friend like Thee—
A friend to soothe and sympathise,
  A friend to care for me.
I need the heart of Jesus,
  To feel each anxious care,
To tell my every want,
  And all my sorrows share.

I need Thee, precious Jesus!
  For I am very blind;
A weak and foolish wanderer,
  With a dark and evil mind.
I need the light of Jesus,
  To tread the thorny road,
To guide me safe to glory,
  Where I shall see my God.

I need Thee, precious Jesus !
  I need Thee day by day,
To fill me with Thy fulness,
  To lead me on my way.
I need Thy Holy Spirit,
  To teach me what I am,
To show me more of Jesus,
  To point me to the Lamb.

I need Thee, precious Jesus !
  And hope to see Thee soon,
Encircled with the rainbow,
  And seated on Thy throne ;
There, with Thy blood-bought children,
  My joy shall ever be,
To sing Thy praises, Jesus !
  To gaze, my Lord, on Thee !

The Christian and his Echo.

TRUE faith, producing love to God and man,
Say, Echo, is not this the Gospel plan ?
      The Gospel plan.

Must I my faith and love to Jesus show,
By doing good to all, both friend and foe ?
      Both friend and foe.

But if a brother hates and treats me ill,
Must I return him good, and love him still?
   Love him still.

If he my failings watches to reveal,
Must I his faults as carefully conceal?
   As carefully conceal.

But if my name and character he blast,
And cruel malice, too, a long time last;
And if I sorrow and affliction know,
He loves to add unto my cup of woe;
In this uncommon, this peculiar case,
Sweet Echo, say, must I still love and bless?
   Still love and bless.

Whatever usage ill I may receive,
Must I be patient still, and still forgive?
   Be patient still, and still forgive.

Why, Echo, how is this? thou'rt sure a dove!
Thy voice shall teach me nothing else but love!
   Nothing else but love.

Amen! with all my heart, then be it so;
'Tis all delightful, just, and good, I know;
And now to practise I'll directly go.
   Directly go.

Things being so, whoever me reject,
My gracious God me surely will protect.
          Surely will protect.

Henceforth I'll roll on Him my every care,
And then both friend and foe embrace in prayer.
          Embrace in prayer.

But after all those duties I have done,
Must I, in point of merit, them disown,
And trust for heaven through Jesus' blood alone?
          Through Jesus' blood alone.

Echo, enough! thy counsels to mine ear
Are sweeter than, to flowers, the dew-drop tear;
Thy wise instructive lessons please me well:
I'll go and practise them.   Farewell, farewell!
          PRACTISE them.   Farewell, farewell!

Less and More.

Two prayers, dear Lord, in one—
    Give me both less and more!
Less of the impatient world, and more of Thee;
    Less of myself, and all that heretofore
Made me to slip where willing feet do run,
And held me back from where I fain would be—
    Kept me, my Lord, from Thee!

All things which most I need
  Are Thine ; Thou wilt bestow
Both strength and shield, and be my willing
    Guest.
  Yet my weak heart takes up a broken reed,
Thy rod and staff doth readily forego :
And I, who might be rich, am poor, distressed,
  And seek but have not rest.

How long, O Lord, how long ?
  So have I cried of late,
As though I knew not what I well do know
  Come, Thou Great Master Builder, and create
Anew that which is Thine ; undo my wrong—
Breathe on this waste, and life and health bestow,
  Come, Lord, let it be so !

Let it be so, and then—
  What then ? My soul shall wait,
And ever pray—all prayers, dear Lord, in one—
  Thy will o'er mine in all this mortal state
Hold regal sway. To Thy commands, Amen !
Break from my waiting lips till work is done,
  And crown and glory won.

Comfort by the Way.

I JOURNEY through a desert drear and wild,
Yet is my heart by such sweet thoughts beguiled,
Of Him on whom I lean—my strength and
　　　stay—
I can forget the sorrows of the way.

Thoughts of His love ! the root of every grace
Which finds in this poor heart a dwelling-place ;
The sunshine of my soul, than day more bright,
And my calm pillow of repose by night.

Thoughts of His sojourn in this vale of tears !
The tale of love unfolded in those years
Of sinless suffering and patient grace,
I love again, and yet again, to trace.

Thoughts of His glory ! on the cross I gaze,
And there behold its sad, yet healing rays ;
Beacon of hope ! which, lifted up on high,
Illumes with heavenly light the tear-dimmed
　　　eye.

Thoughts of His coming !　For that joyful day
In patient hope I watch, and wait, and pray.
The dawn draws nigh, the midnight shadows
　　　flee,
And what a sunrise will that advent be.

Thus, while I journey on my Lord to meet,
My thoughts and meditations are so sweet
Of Him on whom I lean—my strength, my
      stay—
I can forget the sorrows of the way.

—·+·—

Retrospect.

O LOVING ONE! O bounteous One!
   What have I not received from Thee,
Throughout the seasons that have gone
   Into the past eternity!

Lowly my name and mine estate;
   Yet, Father, many a child of Thine,
Of purer heart and cleaner hands,.
   Walks in an humbler path than mine.

And, looking backward through the year,
   Along the way my feet have pressed,
I see sweet places everywhere—
   Sweet places where my soul had rest.

For, though some human hopes of mine
   Are dead, and buried from my sight,
Yet from their graves immortal flowers
   Have sprung, and blossomed into light.

Body, and heart, and soul have been
    Fed by the most convenient food;
My nights are peaceful all the while,
    And all my mortal days are good.

My sorrows have not been so light
    Thy chastening hand I could not trace;
Nor have my blessings been so great
    That they have hid my Father's face.

How doth Death speak of our Beloved?

" The rain that falls upon the height,
    Too gently to be called delight,
    In the dark valley re-appears
    As a wild cataract of tears:
    And love in life shall strive to see
    Sometimes what love in death would be."
                —*Angel in the House.*

How doth Death speak of our beloved,
    When it hath laid them low;
When it has set its hallowing touch
    On speechless lip and brow?

It clothes their every gift and grace
With radiance from the holiest place,
With light as from an angel's face;

Recalling with resistless force,
And tracing to their hidden source,
Deeds scarcely noticed in their course:

This little, loving, fond device,
That daily act of sacrifice,
Of which too late we learn the price !

Opening our weeping eyes to trace
Simple, unnoticed kindnesses,
Forgotten notes of tenderness,

Which evermore to us must be
Sacred as hymns in infancy,
Learned listening at a mother's knee.

Thus doth Death speak of our beloved,
   When it has laid them low ;
Then let Love antedate the work of Death,
   And do this now !

How doth Death speak of our beloved,
   When it has laid them low ;
When it has set its hallowing touch
   On speechless lip and brow ?

It sweeps their faults with heavy hand,
As sweeps the sea the trampled sand,
Till scarce the faintest print is scanned.

It shows how such a vexing deed
Was but generous nature's weed,
Or some choice virtue run to seed ;

How that small, fretting fretfulness
Was but love's over-anxiousness,
Which had not been, had love been less.

This failing, at which we repined,
But the dim shade of day declined,
Which should have made us doubly kind.

Thus doth Death speak of our beloved,
  When it has laid them low;
Then let Love antedate the work of Death,
  And do this now!

———

How doth Death speak of our beloved,
  When it has laid them low;
When it has set its hallowing touch
  On speechless lip and brow?

It takes each failing on our part,
And brands it in upon the heart,
With caustic power and cruel art.

The small neglect that may have pained,
A giant stature will have gained,
When it can never be explained.

The little service which had proved
How tenderly we watched and loved,
And those mute lips to glad smiles moved.

The little gift from out our store,
Which might have cheered some cheerless hour,
When they with earth's poor needs were poor,
But never will be needed more !

It shows our faults like fires at night,
It sweeps their failings out of sight,
It clothes their good in heavenly light.

O Christ, our life ! foredate the work of Death,
    And do this now !
Thou who art Love, thus hallow our beloved—
    Not death, but Thou !

—+—

A Christmas Hymn.

IN human form enthroned,
    The sin of man atoned,
Immanuel sits in highest seat of heaven ;
    Our nature there He wears,
    And that blest union bears,
In David's city on the low earth given.

    He draws us by a love,
    Not such as seraphs move
In happy life through all the realms of space ;
    More subtle is the chord—
    The speaking of a word,
In language learned among our fleshly race.

K

"My blood, once flowing free
Upon the darkened tree,
Gives life to you in heaven's eternal room ;
The Brother and the Friend,
Through ages without end,
Shall e'en outlast the Saviour from the doom."

———⊷———

The Way, the Truth, and the Life.

THOU art the Way!
All ways are thorny mazes without Thee ;
Where hearts are pierced, and thoughts all
aimless stray,
In Thee the heart stands firm, the life moves
free :
Thou art our Way!

Thou art the Truth!
Questions the ages break against in vain
Confront the spirit in its untried youth ;
It starves while learning poison from the grain :
Thou art the Truth!

Thou art the Truth!
Truth for the mind, grand, glorious, infinite !
A heaven still boundless o'er its highest
growth ;
Bread for the heart its daily need to meet.
Thou art the Truth!

Thou art the Light!
Earth beyond earth no faintest ray can give;
  Heaven's shadeless noontide blinds our
    mortal sight;
In Thee we look on God, and love and live:
    Thou art our Light!

Thou art the Rock!
Doubts none can solve heave wild on every side,
  Wave meeting wave of thought in ceaseless
    shock;
On Thee the soul rests calm amidst the tide:
    Thou art the Rock!

Thou art the Life!
All ways without Thee paths that end in death;
  All life without Thee with death's harvest
    rife;
All truths dry bones, disjoined and void of
  breath:
    Thou art our Life!

For Thou art Love!
Our Way and End! the way is rest with Thee!
  O living Truth! the truth is life in Thee!
O Life essential! life is bliss with Thee!
    For Thou art Love!

The Time for Prayer.

WHEN is the time for prayer?
   With the first beams that light the morning
      sky,
Ere for the toils of day thou dost prepare,
   Lift up thy thoughts on high;
Commend thy loved ones to His watchful care:
   Morn is the time for prayer.

And in the noontide hour,
   If worn by toil, or by sad cares oppressed,
Then unto God thy spirit's sorrow pour,
   And He will give thee rest;
Thy voice shall reach Him through the fields
      of air:
   Noon is the time for prayer.

When the bright sun hath set,
   While eve's bright colours deck the skies—
When with the loved at home again thou'st met,
   Then let thy prayers arise
For those who in thy joys and sorrows share:
   Eve is the time for prayer.
And when the stars come forth—
   When to the trusting heart sweet hopes are
      given,
And the deep stillness of the hour gives birth
   To pure bright dreams of heaven,

Kneel to thy God—ask strength life's ills to
    bear :
    Night is the time for prayer.

When is the time for prayer ?
    In *every hour*, while life is spared to thee ;
In crowds or solitude, in joy or care,
    Thy thoughts should heavenward flee.
At home, at morn and eve, with loved ones
    there,
    Bend thou the knee in prayer !

———⨯———

Light in Darkness.

BREEZES of spring, all earth to life awaking,
    Birds swiftly soaring through the sunny sky,
The butterfly its lonely prison breaking,
    The seed up-springing which had seemed to
    die :

Types such as these a word of hope have
    spoken,
    Have shed a gleam of light around the
    tomb ;
But weary hearts longed for a surer token,
    A clearer ray, to dissipate its gloom.

And this was granted !   See the Lord ascending
    On crimson clouds of evening calmly borne,

With hands outstretched, and looks of love still
    bending
    On His bereaved ones, who no longer mourn.

"I am the resurrection!" hear Him saying;
    "I am the life; he who believes in me
Shall never die; the souls my call obeying,
    Soon where I am for evermore shall be."

Sing Halleluiah! light from heaven appearing,
    The mystery of life and death is plain;
Now to the grave we can descend unfearing,
    In sure and certain hope to rise again!

—⤬—

Communion with God.

LORD! I am come along with Thee,
Thy voice to hear, Thy face to see,
    And feel Thy presence near.
It is not fancy's lovely dream,
Though wondrous e'en to faith it seem,
    That Thou dost wait me here.

A moment from this outward life,
Its service, self-denial, strife,
    I joyfully retreat;
My soul, through intercourse with Thee,
Strengthened, refreshed, and calmed shall be,
    Its scenes again to meet.

How can it be that one so mean,
A sinner, selfish, dark, unclean,
  Thus in the holiest stands?
And in that light divinely pure
Which may no stain of sin endure,
  Lifts up rejoicing hands!

Jesus! the answer Thou hast given!
Thy death, Thy life, have opened heaven
  And all its joys to me;
Washed in Thy blood—oh, wondrous grace!—
I'm holy as the holy place
  In which I worship Thee.

How sweet, how solemn thus to lie,
And feel Jehovah's searching eye
  On me well pleased can rest!
Because with His Beloved Son
The Father's grace has made me *one,*
  I must be always blest.

The secret pangs I could not tell
To dearest friend—*Thou* knowest well;
  They claim Thy gracious heart:
Thou dost remove with tender care,
Or sweetly give me strength to bear
  The sanctifying smart.

Thy presence has a wondrous power!
The sharpest thorn becomes a flower,
  And breathes a sweet perfume;

Whate'er looked dark and sad before,
With happy light shines silvered o'er,
  There's no such thing as gloom !

Thou know'st I have a cross to bear ;
The needful stroke Thou dost not spare,
  To keep me near Thy side ;
But when I see the chastening rod
In Thy pierced hand, my Lord, my God !
  I feel so satisfied !

Now, while I tell Thee how, within,
I oft indulge my bosom sin,
  How faithless oft I prove ;
No cold repulse, no frown I meet,
But tender, soul-subduing, sweet
  Is the rebuke of Love.

The Sufferer Cheered.

" SAY ! shall I take the thorn away ? "——
 So spake my gracious Lord——
" O'er which thy sighs are heaved by day,
 Thy nightly tears are poured ?
Say ! shall I give thee rest and ease,
 Make earth's fair prospects rise,
And bid thy bark o'er summer seas
  Float smoothly to the skies ?

" Shall peace and plenty's cup swell high,
  Health leap through every vein,
And all exempt thy moments fly
  From bitter inward pain ?
Be naught to check the inspiring flow
  Of human friendship's tide ;
And every want thy heart can know,
  Be quickly satisfied ?

"Know, thine ease-loving heart might miss
  The *comfort* with the *care !*
And that full tide of earthly bliss
  Leave little room for prayer !
Few were thy visits to the throne,
  Unhastened there by pain ;
Thou, o'er thy bosom-sins, alone,
  Wouldst small advantage gain !

" Nor deem the highest, holiest joy
  A stranger still to woe ;
Blest servants in my high employ,
  Most closely linked they go.
My love illumes with tenderest rays
  The path of self-denial ;
And burning bright the glory's blaze
  That crowns the fiery trial !

" In conscious weakness thou shalt hang
  On my almighty arm !
Soon as the thorn inflicts its pang,
  I'll pour my love's rich balm.

Thou 'plainest in thy deepest woe
  Shalt feel me at thy side ;
And, for my praise, to all shalt show
  Thou art well satisfied.

" Then, wilt thou in thy Master's cup
  Consent awhile to share ?
Know, when in love I drank it up,
  No *wrath* was left thee there !
Thy Saviour's love and power to bless,
  Trust where thou canst not *see !*
And in yon howling wilderness
  Step fearless forth with me ! "

" Lord ! magnify Thyself in me ! "
  With faltering lips I said ;
For, strong to bear as faith may be,
  Weak nature quails with dread.
But He who through the shrinking flesh
  The spirit's will can read,
Smiled on His work, and bade afresh
  ALL GRACE MEET ALL MY NEED.

All in Christ.

In Thee my heart, O Jesus! finds repose;
   Thou bringest rest to all that weary are.
Until that Day-spring from on high arose,
   I wandered through a night without a star;
      My feet had gone astray
      Upon a lonely way:
Each guide I followed failed me in my need;
Each staff I leaned on proved a broken reed.

Then when, in mine extremity, to Thee
   I turned, Thy pity did prevent my prayer;
From that entangling maze it set me free,
   And quickly loosed my heavy load of care;
      Gave me the lofty scope
      Of a heaven-centred hope, .
And led me on with Thee, a gentle Guide,
Thither, where pure immortal joys abide.

Thou art the great completion of my soul,
   The blest fulfilment of its deepest need;
When, self-surrendered to Thy mild control,
   It enters into liberty indeed;
      Thy love, a genial law,
      Its every aim doth draw
Within its holy range, and sweetly lure
Its longings toward the beautiful and pure.

Thy presence is the never-failing spring
　　Of life and comfort in each darker hour ;
And, through Thy grace, benignly ministering,
　　Grief wields a secret, purifying power.
　　　　'Tis sweet, O Lord ! to know
　　　　Thy kindredness with woe ;
Sweeter to walk with Thee on ways apart,
Than with the world, where heart is shut to
　　　heart.

For thee eternity reserves her hymn ;
　　For thee earth has her prayers, and heaven
　　　her vows ;
Thy saints adore Thee, and the seraphim
　　Under Thy glory stoop their starry brows.
　　　　Oh ! may that light divine
　　　　On me still clearer shine—
A power, an inspiration from above,
Lifting me higher to Thy perfect love !

—▸◂—

"𝔥imself batb 𝔇one it !"

" HIMSELF hath done it " all !　Oh ! how those
　　words
　　Should hush to silence every murmuring
　　　thought !
Himself hath done it !—He who loves me best,
　　He who my soul with His own blood hath
　　　bought.

"Himself hath done it!" Can it then be aught
    Than full of wisdom, full of tenderest love ?
Not *one* unneeded sorrow will He send,
    To teach this wandering heart no more to
      rove.

"Himself hath done it!" Yes, although severe
    May seem the stroke, and bitter be the
      cup,
'Tis His own hand that holds it, and I know
    He'll give me grace to drink it meekly up.

"Himself hath done it!" Oh! no arm but His
    Could e'er sustain beneath earth's dreary lot ;
But while I know He's doing all things well,
    My heart His loving-kindness questions not.

"Himself hath done it!" He who.'s searched
      me through,
    Sees how I cleave to earth's ensnaring ties ;
And so He breaks each reed on which my soul
    Too much for happiness and joy relies.

"Himself hath done it!" He would have me
      see
    What broken cisterns human friends *must*
      prove ;
That I may turn and quench my burning thirst
    At His own fount of *ever-living* love.

"Himself hath done it!" Then I fain would
    say,
  "Thy will in *all* things evermore be done;"
E'en though that will remove whom best I love,
  While Jesus lives I cannot be alone.

"Himself hath done it!" Precious, precious
    words,
  "Himself," my Father, Saviour, Brother,
    Friend;
Whose faithfulness no variation knows;
  Who, having loved me, loves me *to the end.*

And when, in His eternal presence blest,
  I at His feet my crown immortal cast,
I'll gladly own, with all His ransomed saints,
  "Himself hath done it"—all, from first to
    last!

—————

Living Waters.

IN some wild Eastern legend the story has
  been told,
Of a fair and wondrous fountain, that flowed in
  times of old;
Cold and crystalline its waters, brightly glanc-
  ing in the ray
Of the summer moon at midnight, or the sun
  at height of day.

And a good angel, resting there, once in a
 favoured hour
Infused into the limpid depths a strange, mysterious power;
A hidden principle of life, to rise and gush again,
Where but some drops were scattered on the
 dry and barren plain.

So the traveller might journey, not now in fear
 and haste,
Far through the mountain-desert, far o'er the
 sandy waste,
If but he sought this fountain first, and, from
 its wondrous store,
The secret of unfailing springs along with him
 he bore.

Wild and fanciful the legend—yet may not
 meanings high,
Visions of better things to come, within its
 shadow lie?
Type of a better fountain, to mortals now un-
 sealed,
The full and free salvation in Christ our Lord
 revealed!

Beneath the Cross those waters rise, and he
 who finds them there,
All through the wilderness of life the living
 stream may bear;

And blessings follow in his steps, until, where'er
      he goes,
The moral wastes begin to bud and blossom as
      the rose.

Ho! every one that thirsteth, come to this
      fountain side!
Drink freely of its waters, drink, and be satisfied!
Yet linger not, but hasten on, and bear to all
      around ·
Glad tidings of the love, and peace, and mercy
      thou hast found;

To Afric's pathless deserts, to Greenland's
      frozen shore—
Where din of mighty cities sounds, or savage
      monsters roar—
Wherever man may wander with his heritage
      of woe,
To tell of brighter things above,—go, brothers,
      gladly go!

Then, as of old, in vision seen before the
      prophet's eyes,
Broader and deeper on its course the stream
      of life shall rise;
And everywhere, as on it flows, shall carry
      light and love,
Peace and good-will to man on earth, glory to
      God above!

Abide with us.

THE tender light is fading where
    We pause and linger still,
And, through the dim and saddened air,
    We feel the evening chill.

Long hast Thou journeyed with us, Lord,
    Ere we Thy face did know;
Oh! still Thy fellowship afford,
    While dark the shadows grow.

For passed is many a beauteous field
    Beside our morning road.
And many a fount to us is sealed
    That once so freshly flowed.

The splendour of the noontide lies
    On other paths than ours;
The dews that lave yon fragrant skies
    Will not revive our flowers.

It is not now as in the glow
    Of life's impassioned heat,
When to the heart there seemed to flow
    All that of earth was sweet.

Something has faded—something died—
    Without us and within;
We more than ever need a guide;
    Blinded and weak with sin.

L

The weight is heavy that we bear,
  Our strength more feeble grows:
Weary with toil and pain and care,
  We long for sweet repose.

Stay with us, gracious Saviour, stay,
  While friends and hopes depart!
Fainting, on Thee we wish to lay
  The burden of our heart.

Abide with us, dear Lord! remain
  Our Life, our Truth, our Way!
So shall our loss be turned to gain—
  Night dawn to endless day.

———+———

The Better Life.

" All the way by which the Lord thy God led thee.

WHEN we reach a quiet dwelling
  On the strong eternal hills,
And our praise to Him is swelling,
  Who the vast creation fills;
When the paths of prayer and duty
  And affliction all are trod,
And we wake and see the beauty
  Of our Saviour and our God;

With the light of resurrection
  When our changèd bodies glow,

And we gain the full perfection
  Of the bliss begun below;
When the life that flesh obscureth
  In each radiant form shall shine,
And the joy that aye endureth
  Flashes forth in beams divine;

While we wave the palms of glory
  Through the long eternal years,—
Shall we e'er forget the story
  Of our mortal griefs and fears?
Shall we e'er forget the sadness
  And the clouds that hung so dim,
When our hearts are filled with gladness,
  And our tears are dried by Him?

Shall the memory be banished
  Of His kindness and His care,
When the wants and woes are vanished
  Which He loved to soothe and share?
All the way by which He brought us,
  All the grievings which He bore,
All the patient love He taught us,
  Shall we think of them no more?

Yes! we surely shall remember
  How He quickened us from death;
How He fanned the dying ember
  With His Spirit's glowing breath:

We shall read the tender meaning
    Of the sorrows and alarms
As we trod the desert, leaning
    On His everlasting arms.

And His rest will be the dearer
    When we think of weary ways,
And His light will seem the clearer
    As we muse on cloudy days.
Oh ! 'twill be a glorious morrow
    To a dark and stormy day ;
We shall recollect our sorrow
    As the streams that pass away.

———+<———

Pray for whom Thou lovest.

Pray for whom thou lovest : thou wilt never have any comfort
of his friendship for whom thou dost not pray.

YES, pray for whom thou lovest : thou mayst
    vainly, idly seek
The fervid words of tenderness by feeble words
    to speak.
Go, kneel before thy Father's throne, and
    meekly, humbly there
Ask blessing for the loved one, in the silent
    hour of prayer.

Yes, pray for whom thou lovest: if uncounted
    wealth were thine—
The treasures of the boundless deep, the riches
  . of the mine—
Thou couldst not to thy cherished friends a
    gift so dear impart
. As the earnest benediction of a deeply-loving
    heart.

Seek not the worldling's friendship; it shall
    droop and wane ere long,
In the cold and heartless glitter of the pleasure-
    loving throng;
But seek the friend who, when thy prayer for
    him shall murmured be,
Breathes forth in faithful sympathy a fervent
    prayer for thee.

And should thy flowery path of life become a
    path of pain,
The friendship formed in bonds like these thy
    spirit shall sustain;
Years may not chill, nor change invade, nor
    poverty impair,
The love that grew and flourished at the holy
    time of prayer.

—◦◦—

Drawing Water.

I HAD drank with lip unsated
　　Where the founts of pleasure burst,
I had hewn out broken cisterns,
　　And they mocked my spirit's thirst.

And I said, Life is a desert,
　　Hot and measureless and dry;
And God will not give me water,
　　Though I pray and faint and die!

Spoke there then a friend and brother,
　　"Rise and roll the stone away!
There are founts of life up-springing
　　In thy pathway every day."

Then I said my heart was sinful—
　　Very sinful was my speech;
All the wells of God's salvation
　　Are too deep for me to reach.

And he answered: "Rise and labour!
　　Doubt and idleness is death;
Shape thou out a goodly vessel
　　With the strong hands of thy faith!"

So I wrought and shaped the vessel,
　　Then knelt lowly, humbly there;
And I drew up living water,
　　With the golden chain of prayer.

A True Dream.

I DREAMT we danced in careless glee,
With hearts and footsteps light and free,
That one so dearly loved and I,
As in the childish days gone by
For ever.

I felt her arms around me fold,
I heard her soft laugh as of old ;
Her eyes with smiles were brimming o'er,
Eyes we may meet on earth no more
For ever.

Then there came mingling with my dreams
 A sense perplexed of loss and change—
  An echo dim of time and tears ;
Until I said : "How long it seems
 Since thus we danced ! Is it not strange ?
  Do you not feel the weight of years ?
Or dread life's evening shadows cold ?
Or mourn to think we must grow old ?"
Wondering, she paused a little while,
Then answered, with a radiant smile :
"No, never !"

Wondering as if to her I told
 The customs of some foreign land,

Or spoke a tongue she knew of old,
   But could no longer understand.
Till o'er her face that sunshine broke,
And with that radiant smile she spoke
                That " Never."

But not until the dream had fled
I knew the sense of what she said :
Young with immortal truth and love,
Child in the Father's house above
                For ever.

We echo back thy words again ;
They smite us with no grief or pain ;
We journey not towards the night,
But to the breaking of the light
                Together.

Our life is no poor cisterned store
   The lavish years are draining low ;
But living streams, that welling o'er,
   Fresh from the Living Fountain flow
                For ever.

"O Lord! Thou knowest."

THOU knowest, Lord, the weariness and sor-
  row
  Of the sad heart that comes to Thee for
    rest ;
Cares of to-day, and burdens for to-morrow,
  Blessings implored, and sins to be confessed :
I come before Thee at Thy gracious word,
And lay them at Thy feet—Thou knowest,
    Lord.

Thou knowest all the past ; how long and
    blindly
  On the dark mountains the lost wanderer
    strayed ;
How the Good Shepherd followed, and how
    kindly
  He bore it home, upon His shoulders laid,
And healed the bleeding wounds, and soothed
    the pain ;
And brought back life and hope and strength
    again.

Thou knowest all the present : each temptation,
  Each toilsome duty, each foreboding fear ;
All to myself assigned of tribulation,
  Or to belovèd ones, than self more dear !
All pensive memories, as I journey on,
Longings for vanished smiles, and voices gone !

Thou knowest all the future; gleams of glad-
    ness,
  By stormy clouds too quickly overcast;
Hours of sweet fellowship, and parting sadness,
  And the dark river to be crossed at last.
Oh! what could confidence and hope afford
To tread that path, but this—*Thou knowest,
    Lord!*

Thou knowest, not alone as God, all-knowing;
  As man, our mortal weakness Thou hast
    proved;
On earth, with purest sympathies o'erflowing,
  O Saviour! Thou hast wept, and Thou hast
    loved!
And Love and Sorrow still to Thee may come,
And find a hiding-place, a rest, a home.

Therefore I come, Thy gentle call obeying,
  And lay my sins and sorrows at Thy feet,
On everlasting strength my weakness staying,
  Clothed in Thy robe of righteousness com-
    plete
Then rising and refreshed, I leave Thy throne,
And follow on to know as I am known!

Ministry.

"The Son of Man came not to be ministered unto, but to
minister."

SINCE service is the highest lot,
    And all are in one body bound,
In all the world the place is not
    Which may not with this bliss be crowned.

The sufferer on the bed of pain
    Need not be laid aside from this ;
But for each kindness gives again
    "This joy of doing kindnesses."

The poorest may enrich this feast ;
    Not one lives only to receive,
But renders, through the hands of Christ,
    Richer returns than man can give.

The little child, in trustful glee,
    With love and gladness brimming o'er,
Many a cup of ministry
    May for the weary veteran pour.

The lonely glory of a throne
    May yet this lowly joy preserve ;
Love may make that a stepping-stone,
    And raise " I reign " into " I serve."

This, by the ministries of prayer,
  The loneliest life with blessings crowds,
Can consecrate each petty care,
  Make angels' ladders out of clouds.

Nor serve we only when we gird
  Our hearts for special ministry ;
That creature best has ministered
  Which is what it was meant to be.

Birds by being glad their Maker bless,
  By simply shining, sun and star ;
And we, whose law is love, serve less
  By what we do than what we are.

Since service is the highest lot,
  And angels know no higher bliss,
Then with what good her cup is fraught
  Who was created but for this !

— ⋅∗⋅ —

It is well.

So they said, who saw the wonders
  Of Messiah's power and love ;
So they sing, who see His glory
  In the Father's house above ;
Ever reading, in each record
  Of the strangely varied past,

"All was well which God appointed,
  All has wrought for good at last."

And on earth we hear the echoes
  Of that chorus in the sky;
Through the day of toil or weeping,
  Faith can raise a glad reply.
It is well, O saints departed!
  Well with you, for ever blest;
Well with us, who journey forward
  To your glory and your rest!

Times are changing, days are flying,
  Years are quickly past and gone;
While the wildly mingled murmur
  Of life's busy hum goes on;
Sounds of tumult, sounds of triumph,
  Marriage chimes and passing-bell;
Yet through all one key-note sounding,
  Angels' watchword: "It is well."

We may hear it through the rushing
  Of the midnight tempest's wave;
We may hear it through the weeping
  Round the newly-covered grave,
In the dreary house of mourning;
  In the darkened room of pain,
If we listen meekly, rightly,
  We may catch that soothing strain.

For Thine arm Thou hast not shortened,
  Neither turned away Thine ear,
O Saviour ! ever ready
  The afflicted's prayer to hear !
Show us light, still surely resting
  Over all Thy darkest ways ;
Give us faith, still surely trusting
  Through the sad and evil days.

And thus, while years are fleeting,
  Though our joys are with them gone,
In Thy changeless love rejoicing
  We shall journey calmly on ;
Till at last, all sorrow over,
  Each our tale of grace shall tell
In the heavenly chorus joining :
  " Lord, Thou hast done all things well!"

———

I.

The Cross.

" Now there stood by the cross of Jesus, His mother."

THE strongest light casts deepest shade,
  The dearest love makes dreariest loss,
And she His birth so blessed had made
  Stood by Him dying on the cross.

Yet since not grief but joy shall last,
    The day and not the night abide,
And all time's shadows, earthward cast,
    Are lights upon the "other side;"

Through what long bliss that shall not fail,
    That darkest hour shall brighten on!
Better than any angel's "*Hail!*"
    The memory of "*Behold thy Son!*"

Blessed in thy lowly heart to store
    The homage paid at Bethlehem;
But far more blessèd evermore,
    Thus to have shared the taunts and shame;

Thus with thy pierced heart to have stood
    'Mid mocking crowds and owned Him
        thine,
True through a world's ingratitude,
    And owned in death by lips Divine.

—⊷—

II.

The Crown.

THOU shalt be crowned, O mother blest!
    Our hearts behold thee crowned e'en now;
The crown of motherhood, earth's best,
    O'ershadowing thy maiden brow.

Thou shalt be crowned!   More fragrant bays
   Than ever poet's brows entwine,
For thine immortal hymn of praise,
   First Singer of the Church, are thine.

Thou shalt be crowned!   All earth and heaven
   Thy coronation pomp shall see ; .
The Hand by which thy crown is given
   Shall be no stranger's hand to thee.

Thou shalt be crowned! but not a queen ;
   A better triumph ends thy strife :
Heaven's bridal raiment, white and clean,
   The victor's crown of fadeless life.

Thou shalt be crowned! but not alone—
   No lonely pomp shall weigh thee down ;
Crowned with the myriads round His throne,
   And casting at His feet thy crown.

—•—

Prayer out of the Depths.

ALL in weakness, all in sorrow,
   O my God! I come once more,
Lifting up the sad petition
   Thou hast often heard before,
In the former days of darkness,
   In the time of need of yore.

For a present help in trouble
   Thou hast never ceased to be,
Since at first a weeping sinner
   Fell before Thee trustingly ;
And Thy voice is ever sounding :
   " O ye weary ! come to me."

Lord, Thou knowest all the weakness
   Of the creatures Thou hast made,
For with mortal imperfection
   Thou didst once Thy glory shade ;
Thou hast loved and Thou hast sorrowed,
   In the veil of flesh arrayed.

Thus I fear not to approach Thee
   With my sorrow and my care ;
Hear my mourning supplication,
   Cast not out my humble prayer !
Lay not on a greater burden
   Than Thy feeble child can bear !

Earth has lost its best attractions,
   All the brightest stars are gone—
All is clouded now and cheerless,
   Where so long a glory shone :
Where I walked with loved companions,
   I must wander now alone.

All is dark on the horizon,
   Clouds returning after rain ;

Faith is languid, Hope is weary,
  And the questions rise again :
" Doth the promise fail for ever ?
  Hast Thou made all men in vain ? "

O my God ! rebuke the tempter ;
  Let not unbelief prevail !
Pray for me, Thy feeble servant,
  ·That my weak faith may not fail,
Nor my Hope let go her anchor
  When the waves and storms assail !

All these passing, changing shadows,
  All these brief, bright joys below—
Let me grasp them not so closely,
  Nor desire nor prize them so !
Nor endure this bitter anguish
  When Thou bidst me let them go !

O Redeemer ! shall one perish
  Who has looked to Thee for aid ?
Let me see Thee, let me hear Thee,
  Through the gloomy midnight shade ;
Let me hear Thy voice of comfort :
  " It is I ; be not afraid ! "

For when feeling *Thou* art near me,
  All my loneliness is o'er,

And the tempter's dark suggestions
 Can oppress my soul no more ;
I shall dread the path no longer
 Where Thyself hast gone before.

And the lights of earth all fading,
 I can gaze on tearlessly,
When the glory that excelleth,
 When the light of life I see.
Whom besides, in earth or heaven,
 Should my heart desire, but Thee ?

—⚓—

$\mathfrak{Salome.}$

SHE knew not what for them she sought,
 At His right hand and left to sit !
How great the glory, passing thought ;
 How rough the path that led to it.

They knew not what of Him they asked !
 But He their deeper sense distilled.
Gently the selfish wish unmasked,
 But all the prayer of love fulfilled.

Pride sought to lift herself on high,
    And heard but of the bitter cup;
Love would but to her Lord be nigh,
    And won her measure full—heaped up

With vision of His glory blessed;
    Stood on the mountain by His side;
Leaned, at the Supper, on His breast;
    Stood close beneath Him when He died.

One brother shared His cup of woe—
    The second of His martyr-band:
One, by His glory smitten low,
    Rose at the touch of His right hand.

Thus, when by earth's cross lights perplexed,
    We crave the thing that should not be,
God, reading right our erring text,
    Gives what we would ask, could we see.

Memories.

WHEN fall the evening shadows, long and
    deep, across the hill ;
When all the air is fragrance, and all the
    breezes still ;

When the summer sun seems pausing above
    the mountain's brow,
As if he left reluctantly a scene so lovely now ;

Then I linger on the pathway, and I fondly
    gaze and long,
As if reading some old story those deep purple
    clouds among ;

Then Memory approaches, holding up her
    magic glass,
Pointing to familiar figures, which across the
    surface pass.

And often do I question, as I view that phantom
    train,
Whether most with joy or sadness I behold
    them thus again.

They are there, those scenes of beauty, where
    life's brightest hours have fled,
And I haste, with dear companions, the old
    paths again to tread ;

But, suddenly dissolving, all the loveliness is
    flown,
And I find a thorny wilderness, where I must
    walk alone.

Thou art there, so loved and honoured, as in
    each former hour,
When we read thine eye's deep meaning, when
    we heard thy words of power ;

When our souls, as willing captives, have sought
    to follow thine,
Tracing the eternal footsteps of Might and
    Love Divine.

But o'er that cherished image falls a veil of
    clouds and gloom,
And beside a bier I tremble, or I weep above
    a tomb.

And ever will the question come, O Memory !
    again,
Whether in thy magic mirror there is most of
    bliss or pain ?

Would I not wish the brightness were for ever
    hid from view,
If but those hours of darkness could be all
    forgotten too?

Then, weary and desponding, my spirit seeks
    to rise
Away from earthly conflicts, from mortal smiles
    or sighs.

I do not think the blessed ones with Jesus have
    forgot
The changing joys and sorrows which have
    marked their earthly lot;

But now, on Memory's record their eyes can
    calmly dwell;
They can see, what here they trusted—God
    hath done all things well;

And vain regrets and longings are as old things
    passed away;
No shadows dim the sunshine of that bright
    eternal day!

The Widow of Nain.

THY miracles are no state splendours
  Whose pomps Thy daily works excel;
The rock which breaks the stream but renders
  Its constant current audible.

The power which startles us in thunders
  Works ever silently in light;
And mightier than these special wonders
  The wonders daily in our sight.   .

Rents in the veils Thy works that fold,
  They let the inner light shine through;
The rent is new, the light is old,
  Eternal ever, ever new.

And, therefore, when Thy touch arrests,
  The bearers of that bier at Nain,
Warm on unnumbered hearts it rests,
  Though yet their dead live not again.

And Thy compassionate "Weep not!"
  On this our tearful earth once heard,
For every age with comfort fraught,
  Tells how Thy heart is ever stirred.

Nature repeats the tale each year,
   She feels Thy touch through countless
      springs,
And, rising from her wintry bier,
   Throws off her grave-clothes, lives and sings.

And when Thy touch through earth shall thrill
   This bier whereon our race is laid,
And, for the first time standing still,
   The long procession of the dead

At Thy " Arise ! " shall wake from clay,
   Young, deathless, freed from every stain ;
When Thy " Weep not ! " shall wipe away
   Tears that shall never come again ;

When the strong chains of death are burst
   And lips long dumb begin to speak,
What name will each then utter first ?
   What music shall that silence break ?

Pathways of the Holy Land.

THE pathways of Thy land are little changed
  Since Thou wert there ;
The busy world through other ways has ranged,
  And left these bare.

The rocky path still climbs the glowing steep
  Of Olivet ;
Though rains of two millenniums wear it deep,
  Men tread it yet.

Still to the gardens o'er the brook it leads,
  Quiet and low ;
Before his sheep the shepherd on it treads—
  His voice they know.

The wild fig throws broad shadows o'er it still,
  As once o'er Thee ;
Peasants go home at evening up that hill
  To Bethany.

And as when gazing Thou didst weep o'er
  them,
  From height to height
The white roofs of discrowned Jerusalem
  Burst on our sight.

These ways were strewed with garments once,
    and palm,
      Which we tread thus ;
Here, through Thy triumph, on Thou passedst,
    calm,
      On to Thy cross.

The waves have washed fresh sands upon the
    shore
      Of Galilee ;
But, chiselled in the hill-sides, evermore
      Thy paths we see.

Man has not changed them in that slumbering
    land,
      Nor time effaced ;
Where Thy feet trod to bless, we still may
    stand—
      All can be traced.

Yet we have traces of Thy footsteps far
      Truer than these ;
Where'er the poor, and tried, and suffering are,
      Thy steps faith sees.

Nor with fond sad regrets Thy steps we
    trace ;
      Thou art not dead !
Our path is onward, till we see Thy face,
      And hear Thy tread.

And now, wherever meets Thy lowliest band
In praise and prayer,
There is Thy presence, there Thy Holy Land,
Thou, Thou, art there !

———+———

For the New Year.

ANOTHER year ! another year
Has borne its record to the skies.
Another year ! another year,
Untried, unproved, before us lies.
We hail with smiles its dawning ray—
How shall we meet its final day ?

Another year, another year !
Its squandered hours will ne'er return.
Oh ! many a heart must quail with fear
O'er memory's blotted page to turn.
No record from that leaf will fade,
Not one erasure may be made.

Another year, another year !
How many a grief has marked its flight!
Some whom we love no more are here—
Translated to the realms of light.
Ah ! none can bless the coming year
Like those no more to greet us here.

Another year, another year !
  Oh ! many a blessing, too, was given,
Our lives to deck, our hearts to cheer,
  And antedate the joys of heaven ;
But they, too, slumber in the past,
Where joys and griefs must sink at last.

Another year, another year !
  Gaze we no longer on the past,
Nor let us shrink, with faithless fear,
  From the dark shade the future casts.
The past, the future—what are they
  To those whose lives may end to-day ?

Another year, another year !
  Perchance the last of life below,
Who, ere its close, Death's call may hear,
  None but the Lord of life can know.
Oh ! to be found, whene'er that day
May come, prepared to pass away.

Another year, another year !
  Help us earth's thorny path to tread ;
So may each moment bring us near
  To Thee, ere yet our lives are fled.
Saviour ! we yield ourselves to Thee,
For time and for eternity.

The Perpetuity of Joy in Heaven.

HERE brief is the sighing,
And brief is the crying,
   For brief is the life !
The life there is endless,
The joy there is endless,
   And ended the strife.

What joys are in heaven ?
To whom are they given ?
   Ah ! what ? and to whom ?
The stars to the earth-born,
" Best robes " to the sin-worn,
   The crown for the doom !

Oh, country the fairest !
Our country the dearest,
   We press toward thee !
O Sion the golden !
Our eyes now are holden,
   Thy light till we see :

Thy crystalline ocean,
Unvexed by commotion,
   Thy fountain of life ;
Thy deep peace unspoken,
Pure, sinless, unbroken—
   Thy peace beyond strife :

Thy meek saints all glorious,
Thy martyrs victorious,
   Who suffer no more ;
Thy halls full of singing,
Thy hymns ever ringing
   Along thy safe shore.

Like the lily for whiteness,
Like the jewel for brightness,
   Thy vestments, O Bride !
The Lamb ever with thee,
The Bridegroom is with thee—
   With thee to abide !

We know not, we know not,
All human words show not,
   The joys we may reach ;
The mansions preparing,
The joys for our sharing,
   The welcome for each.

O Sion the golden !
My eyes still are holden,
   Thy light till I see ;
And deep in thy glory,
Unveiled then before me,
   My King, look on thee.

Through the Flood on Foot.

THE sun had sunk in the west
    For a little while,
And the clouds which gathered to see
      him die
    Had caught his dying smile.

We sat in the door of our tent,
    In the cool of the day,
Toward the quiet meadow
    Where misty shadows lay.

The great and terrible land
    Of wilderness and drought,
Lay in the shadows behind us,
    For the Lord had brought us out.

The great and terrible river,
    Though shrouded still from view,
Lay in the shadows before us,
    But the Lord would bear us through.

In the stillness and the starlight,
    In sight of the Blessed Land,

We thought of the bygone desert-life,
  And the burning, blinding sand.

Many a dreary sunset,
  Many a dreary dawn,
We had watched upon those desert hills
  As we pressed slowly on.

Yet sweet had been the silent dews
  Which from God's presence fell,
And the still hours of resting
  By palm-tree and by well,

Till we pitched our tent at last,
  The desert done,
Where we saw the hills of the Holy Land
  Gleam in our sinking sun ;

And we sat in the door of our tent,
  In the cool of the day,
Toward the quiet meadow
  Where misty shadows lay.

We were talking about the King,
  And our Elder Brother,
As we were used often to speak
  One to another :

The Lord standing quietly by,
   In the shadows dim,
Smiling perhaps, in the dark, to hear
   Our sweet, sweet talk of Him.

"I think in a little while,"
   I said at length,
"We shall see His face in the city
   Of everlasting strength;

"And sit down under the shadow
   Of His smile,
With great delight and thanksgiving,
   To rest awhile."

"But the river—the awful river
   In the dying light!"
And even as he spoke, the murmur
   Of a river rose on the night!

And One came up through the meadow,
   Where the mists lay dim,
Till He stood by my friend in the starlight,
   And spake to him:

"I have come to call thee home,"
   Said our veilèd Guest;

" The terrible journey of life is done,
   I will take thee into rest.

" Arise ! thou shalt come to the palace,
   To rest thee for ever ; "
And He pointed across the dark meadow,
   And down to the river.

And my friend rose up in the shadows,
   And turned to me :
" Be of good cheer," I said, faintly,
   " For He calleth thee."

For I knew by His loving voice,
   His kingly word,
The veilèd Guest in the starlight dim
   Was Christ, the Lord !

So we three went slowly down
   To the river-side,
Till we stood in the heavy shadows
   By the black, wild tide.

I could hear that the Lord was speaking
   Deep words of grace,

I could see their blessed reflection
    On my friend's pale face.

The strong and desolate tide
    Was hurrying wildly past,
As he turned to take my hand once more
    And say Farewell, at last.

" Farewell—I cannot fear.
    Oh ! seest *thou* His grace ?"
And even as he spoke, he turned
    Again to the Master's face.

So they two went closer down
    To the river-side, .
And stood in the heavy shadows
    By the black, wild tide.

But when the feet of the Lord   .
    Were come to the waters dim,
They rose to stand, on either hand,
    And left a path for Him ;

So they two passed over swiftly
    ˙ Toward the goal,
But the wistful, longing gaze
    Of the passing soul

Grew only more rapt and joyful
    As he clasped the Master's hand;
I think, or ever he was aware
    They were come to the Holy Land.

Now I sit alone in the door of my tent
    In the cool of the day,
Toward the quiet meadow
    Where misty shadows play.

The great and terrible land
    Of wilderness and drought,
Lies in the shadows behind me,
    For the Lord hath brought me out;

The great and terrible river
    I stood that night to view,
Lies in the shadows before me,
    But the Lord will bear me through.

The Long Good-Night.

I JOURNEY forth rejoicing,
　　From this dark vale of tears,
To heavenly joy and freedom,
　　From earthly bonds and fears :
Where Christ our Lord shall gather
　　All His redeemed again,
His kingdom to inherit.
　　　　　　Good-night, till then !

Go to thy quiet resting,
　　Poor tenement of clay !
From all thy pain and weakness
　　I gladly haste away ;
But still in faith confiding
　　To find thee yet again,
All glorious and immortal.
　　　　　　Good-night, till then !

Why thus so sadly weeping,
　　Beloved ones of my heart ?
The Lord is good and gracious,
　　Though now He bids us part.
Oft have we met in gladness,
　　And we shall meet again,
All sorrow left behind us.
　　　　　　Good-night, till then !

I go to see His glory,
  Whom we have loved below :
I go, the blessed angels,
  The holy saints to know.
Our lovely ones departed,
  I go to find again,
And wait for you to join us.
                Good-night, till then !

I hear the Saviour calling—
  The joyful hour has come :
The angel-guards are ready
  To guide me to our home,
Where Christ our Lord shall gather
  All His redeemed again,
His kingdom to inherit.
                Good-night, till then !

Footsteps on the other Side.

SITTING in my humble doorway,
 Gazing out into the night,
Listening to the stormy tumult
 With a kind of sad delight—
Wait I for the loved who comes not,
 One whose step I long to hear;
One who, though he lingers from me,
 Still is dearest of the dear.
Soft! he comes—now heart, be quick—
 Leaping in triumphant pride!
Oh! it is a stranger footstep,
 Gone by on the other side.

All the night seems filled with weeping,
 Winds are wailing mournfully;
And the rain-tears together
 Journey to the restless sea.
I can fancy, sea, your murmur,
 As they with your waters flow,
Like the griefs of single beings,
 Making up a nation's woe!

Branches, bid your guests be silent;
 Hush a moment, fretful rain;
Breeze, stop sighing—let me listen,
 God grant not again in vain!

In my cheek the blood is rosy,
 Like the blushes of a bride.
Joy! Alas! a stranger footstep
 Goes by on the other side.

Ah! how many wait for ever
 For the steps that do not come!
Wait until the pitying angels
 Bear them to a peaceful home!
Many in the still of midnight
 In the streets have lain and died,
While the sound of human footsteps
 Went by on the other side.

Gone Home.

GONE home! gone home! She lingers here
  no longer,
 A restless pilgrim, walking painfully,
With homesick longing daily growing stronger,
 And yearning visions of the joys to be.

Gone home! gone home! Her earnest, active
  spirit,
 Her very playfulness, her heart of love!

The heavenly mansion now she doth inherit,
    Which Christ made ready ere she went
       above.

Gone home! gone home! The door through
    which she vanished
Closed with a jar, and left us here alone.
We stand without, in tears, forlorn and
    banished,
    Longing to follow where one loved has
      gone.

Gone home! gone home! Oh! shall we ever
    reach her,
See her again, and know her for our own?
Will she conduct us to the Heavenly Teacher,
    And bow beside us low before His throne?

Gone home! gone home! Oh, human-hearted
    Saviour!
Give us a balm to soothe our heavy woe;
And if Thou wilt, in tender, pitying favour,
    Hasten the time when we may rise and go!

—✦—

𝔉uneral 𝔥ymn.

COME forth, come on, with solemn song :
The road is short, the rest is long,
The Lord brought here, He calls away ;
  Make no delay,
This home was for a passing day.

Here in an inn a stranger dwelt,
Here joy and grief by turns he felt ;
. Poor dwelling ! now we close thy door ;
  The task is o'er,
The sojourner returns no more ;

Now of a lasting home possessed,
He goes to seek a deeper rest.
Good-night ! the day was sultry here
  In toil and fear ;
Good-night ! the night is cool and clear.

Chime on, ye bells ! again begin,
And ring the Sabbath morning in.
The labourer's week-day work is done,
  The rest begun,
Which Christ hath for His people won.

Now open to us, gates of peace ;
Here let the pilgrim's journey cease !
Ye quiet slumberers, make room
    In your still home
For the new stranger who has come !

How many graves around us lie !
How many homes are in the sky !
Yes, for each saint doth Christ prepare
    A place with care.
Thy home is waiting, brother, there.

Jesus, Thou reignest, Lord, alone ;
Thou wilt return and claim Thine own.
Come quickly, Lord ! return again !
    Amen ! Amen !
Thine seal us ever, now and then !

We are the Lord's.

WE are the Lord's: His, earthly life and
    spirit!
  We are the Lord's, who once for all men
    died!
We are the Lord's, and shall all things inherit!
  We are the Lord's, who wins us all beside!

We are the Lord's! So in most holy living,
  Glad let us, body, soul, be His alone;
And heart and mouth and act join, witness
    giving
  That it is surely true: we are His own!

We are the Lord's! So in the dark vale
    gleaming
One star dispels our fear, and, keeping ward,
Doth light our way with sweet unchangeful
    beaming:
  It is the precious Word: We're Thine, O
    Lord!

We are the Lord's! So will He, on the
    morrow,
  Watch our last pang, when other help
    rewards,

No pain, and Death brings not a touch of
    sorrow,
    This . Word's for ever true : We are the
      Lord's !

—⊶—

Euthanasy.

WE need no change of sphere
To view the heavenly sights, or hear
The songs which angels sing.   The hand
    Which gently pressed the sightless orbs ere
      while,
    Giving them light, a world of beauty, and the
      friendly smile,
Can cause our eyes to see the better land.

    We need no wings
    To soar aloft to realms of higher things,
But only feet which walk the paths of peace,
    Guided by Him whose voice
    Greets every ear, makes every heart re-
      joice,
Saying, Arise, and walk where sorrows cease.

    Visiting spirits are near ;
    They are not wholly silent, but we cannot
      hear

Nor understand their speech.
    Our Saviour caught His Father's word,
    And men of old, dreaming and walking, heard
The breathings of a world we cannot reach.

    They mounted to the skies,
    And read deep mysteries.
While yet on earth, they placed a ladder there
    Like Jacob's, that each round should lead,
    By prayer outspoken, in a word or deed,
The soul to heights of clearer, purer air.

    They saw no messenger of gloom
    In him whom we call Death, nor met their doom
As prisoner his sentence ; but naturally, as bud unfolds to flower,
    As child to man, so man to angel—
    They recognising Death the glad evangel,
Leading to higher scenes of life and power.

The Eleventh Hour.

FAINT and worn and aged,
  One stands knocking at a gate,
Though no light shines in the casement,
  Knocking though so late.
It has struck eleven
In the courts of heaven,
  Yet he still doth knock and wait.

While no answer cometh
  From the heavenly hill,
Blessed angels wonder
  At his earnest will.
Hope and fear but quicken
While the shadows thicken :
  He is knocking, knocking still.

Grim the gate unopened,
  Stands with bar and lock ;
Yet within the unseen Porter
  Hearkens to the knock.
Doing and undoing,
Faint and yet pursuing,
  This man's feet are on the Rock.

With a cry unceasing,
  Knocketh, prayeth he :

" Lord, have mercy on me
    When I cry to thee ! "
With a knock unceasing,
And a cry increasing :
    " O my Lord ! remember me."

Still the Porter standeth,
    Love-constrained He standeth near,
While the cry increaseth
    Of that love and fear :
" Jesus, look upon me !
Christ, hast Thou foregone me?—
    If I must, I perish here."

Faint the knocking ceases,
    Faint the cry and call :
Is he lost indeed for ever,
    Shut without the wall?
Mighty Arms surround him,
Arms that sought and found him,
    Held, withheld, and bore through all.

O celestial mansion !
    Open wide the door :
Crown and robes of whiteness,
    Stone inscribed before,
Flocking angels bear them ;
Stretch thy hand and wear them ;
    Sit thou down for evermore.

"Bringing our Sheaves with us."

THE time for toil is past, and night has come,
  The last and saddest of the harvest eves;
Worn out with labour long and wearisome,
Drooping and faint the reapers hasten home,
  Each laden with his sheaves.

Last of the labourers, Thy feet I gain,
  Lord of the harvest! and my spirit grieves
That I am burdened, not so much with grain
As with a heaviness of heart and brain.
  Master, behold my sheaves!

Few, light, and worthless—yet their trifling
      weight
  Through all my frame a weary aching leaves;
For long I struggled with my hapless fate,
And stayed and toiled till it was dark and late—
  Yet these are all my sheaves!

Full well I know I have more tares than
      wheat—
  Brambles and flowers, dry stalks and
      withered leaves;
Wherefore I blush and weep, as at Thy feet
I kneel down reverently, and repeat,
  "Master, behold my sheaves!"

I know these blossoms, clustering heavily,
    With evening dew upon their folded leaves,
Can claim no value nor utility—
Therefore shall fragrancy and beauty be
    The glory of my sheaves.

So do I gather strength and hope anew ;
    For well I know Thy patient love perceives,
Not what I did, but what I strove to do ;
And though the full, ripe ears be sadly few,
    Thou wilt accept my sheaves.

—·+·—

Knocking.

"Behold I stand at the door and knock."

KNOCKING, knocking, ever knocking?
        Who is there?
'Tis a pilgrim, strange and kingly,
        Never such was seen before ;—
Ah, sweet soul, for such a wonder
        Undo the door.

No ; that door is hard to open ;
Hinges rusty, latch is broken ;
        Bid Him go.
Wherefore, with that knocking dreary
Scare the sleep from one so weary ?
        Say Him,—no.

Knocking, knocking, ever knocking?
      What ! Still there?
Oh, sweet soul, but once behold Him,
With the glory-crownèd hair;
And those eyes, so strange and tender,
      Waiting there;
Open ! open ! once behold Him,—
      Him so fair.

Ah, that door !   Why wilt Thou vex me,
Coming ever to perplex me?
For the key is stiffly rusty,
And the bolt is clogged and dusty;
Many-fingered ivy-vine
Seals it fast with twist and twine;
Weeds of years and years before
Choke the passage of that door.

Knocking ! knocking ! What ! still knock-
      ing ?
      He still there ?
What's the hour ?   The night is waning,—
In my heart a drear complaining,
      And a chilly, sad unrest !
Ah, this knocking !   It disturbs me,
Scares my sleep with dreams unblest !
      Give me rest,
      Rest,—ah, rest !

Rest, dear soul, He longs to give thee;
Thou hast only dreamed of pleasure,
Dreamed of gifts and golden treasure,
Dreamed of jewels in thy keeping,
Waked to weariness of weeping;—
Open to thy soul's one Lover,
And thy night of dreams is over,—
The true gifts He brings have seeming
More than all thy faded dreaming!

Did she open? Doth she? Will she?
So, as wondering we behold,
Grows the picture to a sign,
Pressed upon your soul and mine;
For in every breast that liveth
Is that strange, mysterious door;—
Though forsaken and betangled,
Ivy-gnarled and weed-bejangled,
Dusty, rusty, and forgotten;—
There the piercèd hand still knocketh,
And with ever-patient watching,
With the sad eyes true and tender,
With the glory-crownèd hair,—
Still a God is waiting there.

INDEX TO SUBJECTS.

INDEX TO FIRST LINES.

—⊣⊢—

Printed by BALLANTYNE, HANSON & CO., Edinburgh

WORKS BY THE RT. REV. E. H. BICKERSTETH, D.D.,

Bishop of Exeter.

The Master's Home-Call; or, Brief Memorials of Alice Frances Bickersteth. Twenty-fifth Thousand. 1s.

The Master's Will. A Funeral Sermon. Sewn, 6d.; cloth gilt, 1s.

The Reef, and other Parables. With Engravings, 2s. 6d.

The Shadowed Home and the Light Beyond. Eighth Thousand. 5s.

The Shadow of the Rock. A Selection of Religious Poetry. 16mo, cloth extra, 2s. 6d.

Evangelical Churchmanship and Evangelical Electicism. 1s.

The Clergyman in his Home. 1s.

The Hymnal Companion to the Book of Common Prayer. From 1d. to 3s.; with Music, 2s. 6d. to 8s. 6d. Specimen Prospectus and Price List on application.

Chant-Book Companion to the Book of Common Prayer. Edited by CHARLES VINCENT. Price 2s. and 4s.

From Year to Year: Poems and Hymns for all the Sundays and Holy Days of the Church. 16mo, with red border lines, cloth, red edges, 3s. 6d.; parchment, 3s. 6d.; roan, gilt edges, 5s.; padded roan, 6s.; padded calf or morocco, gilt edges, 10s. 6d.

CHOICE EDITIONS OF CHOICE BOOKS. New

Editions. Illustrated by C. W. COPE, R.A.; T. CRESWICK, R.A.; EDWARD DUNCAN, BIRKET FOSTER, J. C. HORSLEY, A.R.A.; GEORGE HICKS, R. REDGRAVE, R.A.; C. STONEHOUSE, F. TAYLER, GEORGE THOMAS, H. J. TOWNSHEND, E. H. WEHNERT, HARRISON WEIR, &c. Crown 8vo, cloth, 2s. 6d. each; morocco, 10s. 6d.

Bloomfield's Farmer's Boy.
Campbell's Pleasures of Hope.
Cundall's Elizabethan Poetry.
Coleridge's Ancient Mariner.
Goldsmith's Deserted Village.
Goldsmith's Vicar of Wakefield.
Gray's Elegy in a Churchyard.

Keat's Eve of St. Agnes.
Milton's l'Allegro.
Roger's Pleasures of Memory.
Shakespeare's Songs & Sonnets.
Tennyson's May Queen.
Weir's Poetry of Nature.
Wordsworth's Pastoral Poems

"Such works are a glorious beatification for a poet."
—*Athenæum.*

LONDON: SAMPSON LOW, MARSTON, SEARLE, & RIVINGTON, LD.

ST. DUNSTAN'S HOUSE,

FETTER LANE, FLEET STREET, E.C.

www.ingramcohtent.com/pod-product-compliance
Lightning Source LLC
Chambersburg PA
CBHW030121030726
47498CB00007B/2488